THE UNINTENTIONAL ADVENTURES OF THE BLAND SISTERS

OF THE

BLAND SISTERS

❖ ❖ Flight of the Bluebird ❖ ❖

by **Kara LaReau** Illustrated by **Jen Hill**

AMULET BOOKS
NEW YORK

Cataloging-in-Publication Data has been applied for and may be obtained from the Library of Congress.

ISBN 978-1-4197-3144-0

Text copyright © 2019 Kara LaReau
Illustrations copyright © 2019 Jen Hill
Book design by Pamela Notarantonio

Printed and bound in U.S.A.
10 9 8 7 6 5 4 3 2 1

Amulet Books are available at special discounts when purchased in quantity for premiums and promotions as well as fundraising or educational use. Special editions can also be created to specification. For details, contact specialsales@abramsbooks.com or the address below.

Amulet Books® is a registered trademark of Harry N. Abrams, Inc.

ABRAMS The Art of Books
195 Broadway, New York, NY 10007
abramsbooks.com

for all my fellow
Daughters
—K.L.

THE UNINTENTIONAL CAST OF CHARACTERS

Jaundice & Kale

Bert

Hattie

Omar

Beatrix

Ricky

Nehy & Nefret

Victor

Uggo

Chapter One

J aundice was going to throw up.

"I'm going to throw up," she said. These words were muffled, as they were spoken through Jaundice's hands, which were pressed over her mouth.

Kale understood her sister immediately. She had herself thrown up a short time ago, when the sisters had been aboard a pirate ship, and she had consumed a significant amount of questionable stew. Now it was Jaundice who looked pale and sweaty.

And now, after their most recent adventure on a certain express train, the Bland Sisters were in an airplane, piloted by a woman sent by their parents to rescue them from some unknown pursuer.

"I'm Beatrix, by the way," the pilot informed them from the cockpit. "Beatrix Airedale."

Beatrix was wearing a leather helmet and goggles, so most of her face was hidden, except for her smile. While Kale found this smile reassuring, Jaundice could only groan.

Unfortunately, throwing up on an airplane is not as easy as throwing up on a ship. On a ship, you can just do it over the railing. Kale looked around frantically for a container. All she could find was what looked like a large, overstuffed backpack.

"Here," she said, handing it to her sister. "Maybe you can throw up in this."

Jaundice offered her mumbled thanks, and managed to keep one hand over her mouth while grabbing the backpack in the other.

"How's everything going back there?" asked Beatrix. The Bland Sisters had only been in the air for a few minutes. It took those few minutes for Jaundice to go from feeling exhilarated, to confused, to nauseated. Kale was still exhilarated.

"It really is quite something," Kale said, looking out the window at the clouds floating below them. Next to her,

Jaundice had just finished retching. "We can't contain our excitement," she added.

"Do you have any . . . water?" Jaundice managed to ask. The pilot reached down and grabbed a canteen. She tossed it to Jaundice, who only barely caught it.

"Not everyone takes to flying right away," Beatrix explained. "I've never been airsick, and I've crashed my plane twice!"

"Twice?" Jaundice said weakly. This news did not instill her—or her stomach—with confidence.

"Well, the first time wasn't exactly a crash. I just ground-looped during my takeoff run, so I ended up colliding with a tractor," the pilot explained. "The crew tried to blame it on me, but it turned out to be a blown tire."

"Ah," said Kale. This made her feel ever-so-slightly better.

"But the second crash was definitely my fault," Beatrix said. "Though I can't feel too bad about it, since that's how I met your parents."

"Our parents?" the Bland Sisters said.

"Whoopsie!" said Beatrix.

At this, the plane shuddered. Jaundice began to moan.

"No worries, kids. Just a bit of turbulence," the pilot explained.

Everything in the plane began to jostle, including the Bland Sisters. Kale felt her head hit the ceiling of the aircraft on more than one occasion. And then, in a few minutes, it stopped.

"See?" said Beatrix. "Easy peasy."

"More like 'easy queasy,'" said Jaundice, holding her stomach.

"It should be a smooth flight from now on," Beatrix promised.

She was right. It was so smooth, in fact, that Jaundice began to feel tired. She imagined her mother was there with her. Lately, the Bland Sisters had been thinking about their parents more than usual, and realized they'd been missing them more than a little. Jaundice felt a distinct ache as she remembered how her mother had taught her and her sister to fall asleep.

"Close your eyes, and imagine you are floating up, up, up an invisible staircase, and into a cozy nest made of feathers and velvet," she would whisper in their ears each night. It worked like a charm.

As Jaundice closed her eyes, she imagined her mother whispering these very things—but not before she pulled out the green scarab she'd slipped into one of her smock pockets before their last adventure. This scarab was coveted by the unknown pursuer who ransacked their house. And this scarab, the Bland Sisters recently learned, allowed them to communicate with their parents in their dreams, as long as they placed it close to their heads. Despite the scarab's distinct lumpiness, Jaundice promptly fell asleep.

In her dream, it was snowing, and very, very cold. Jaundice's teeth chattered as she walked up the steps of what looked like a castle. She opened the door and went in, but once she was inside, she found herself outside again, though in this outside, it was warm and sunny. Her parents were on their hands and knees in a wide field blooming with flowers and plants. Her mother looked like she was digging in the dirt, and her father was looking at Jaundice quite urgently.

He nudged Jaundice's mother. "Look, darling. I think it's Jaundice."

Jaundice's mother looked up and smiled. "It is!" she exclaimed.

As Jaundice looked closer, she could see that her mother wasn't really digging; she was poking at something with a tiny trowel. In her other hand she held a small, thick brush, which she was using to unearth whatever it was she was poking.

"Oh, I wish I could give you a big hug right now, but we can't always control what we do or say in dreams," Jaundice's mother tried to explain.

"And in dreams, a lot of what you see means something else. It's a bit like a game," said her father, shuffling a pack of blank playing cards. "We're hoping you and your sister can figure it out together. There's so much to do, and we have very little time."

"Figure what out?" said Jaundice.

Out of nowhere, a boy and girl appeared. They had very dark skin and hair, and they were wearing beautiful pleated white linen robes with heavy, bejeweled necklaces. They looked at Jaundice and rolled their eyes.

"She has a lot to learn," the boy said to his sister.

"Who are you?" said Jaundice.

"The Sacred Scarabs of the Twins are now in use," the boy said. "When the scarabs are in use, their rightful owners are summoned."

"The scarabs belong to us! Return what was stolen!" said the girl.

"All in good time, children," said Jaundice's mother. "All in good time."

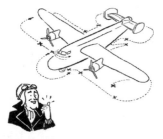

MAKE SURE NO ONE WILL BE STRUCK BY THE ROTATING
PROPELLER BY LOOKING OUT THE WINDOW AND SHOUTING
"CLEAR PROP," THEN ENGAGE THE STARTER. LISTEN TO
THE ROAR OF THE ENGINE AND THE PROPELLER.

TAKING OFF! with Trip Winger

❊ ❊ ❊ ❊ ❊ ❊ Chapter Two ❊ ❊ ❊ ❊ ❊ ❊

W hen Jaundice finally woke up and looked around, she almost expected her parents to be right there next to her. To her disappointment, this was not the case. The plane was still in the air, and outside, the sun seemed to be rising. Had they been flying all night?

Kale was reading a big, thick paperback she'd found near the backpacks; it was called *TAKING OFF! with Trip Winger*, and the author was touted as some sort of aeronautical expert. Kale was always eager for something to read, and the text of this book was perfectly dry, and supplemented by complicated diagrams and illustrations. From the get-go, she was hooked.

"Are you still feeling sick?" Kale asked her sister.

"Ugh," said Jaundice. "Now I feel sick *and* confused."

"We're landing in a few minutes. Evidently, we need to refuel," Kale informed her sister.

Beatrix pulled off her goggles. "I'll meet you at Ricky's after I fuel her up. Breakfast is on me; order me the Barnstormer."

Ricky's, it turned out, was the café in the airport in a place called Casablanca. And
"the Barnstormer" was
a platter of three
pancakes, three
eggs, three pieces of
toast, three slices of
bacon, three pieces
of sausage, three slices
of ham, and a corn
muffin. Two servers
were needed to bring
it to the table.

The Bland
Sisters ordered their
standard breakfast:
oatmeal with weak,
tepid tea.

"I suppose we should wait for Beatrix," Kale said, looking down at her steaming oatmeal bowl.

"It would be the polite thing to do," Jaundice replied. She touched her teacup and frowned. "Besides, it will give everything a chance to cool down. And I can tell you about the dream I had."

Jaundice told Kale about the snow, and the castle, and the field filled with flowers and plants. She told Kale about

seeing their parents, and about the weird way their mother was digging. And she told her sister about the boy and girl in the white robes.

"I can't make heads or tails of it," Jaundice said. She patted the pockets of her smock, which she'd made from an old curtain and the upholstery of a long-since-discarded couch; said pockets were known to contain all manner of seemingly useless items. Jaundice pulled out a long piece of string, with which she began tying and untying knots. The tying and untying helped her think.

"Well, I'm just as confused as you now," Kale admitted. She placed her trusty backpack (which now contained *TAKING OFF! with Trip Winger*, her new favorite read) on the back of her chair. As she did so, she couldn't help noticing the man sitting behind them. He had very large, dark eyes, which seemed to be focused on the Bland Sisters.

"There's a man sitting behind us," Kale whispered to her sister, raising her eyebrows.

"So?" Jaundice asked.

"He's *staring* at us," Kale whispered again.

Jaundice craned her neck to get a better look.

"Don't be so obvious!" Kale warned.

But it was too late. Jaundice locked eyes with the man. He smiled and tipped his hat.

"He's just being friendly," she informed her sister.

13

Beatrix made a grand entrance, greeting all the servers in the café and slapping the cook on the back. When she got to their table, she took off her leather helmet and scarf. It turned out she was very beautiful, with dark skin and very short, black, curly hair. But just as she was beautiful, Beatrix was also all business.

"The Bluebird's ready to go," she announced. "Now it's time for this bird to fuel up."

At this, she began shoveling food into her mouth at an alarming rate. The Bland Sisters took some tentative bites of their oatmeal. It was not as cold or congealed as they would have liked, but they were too hungry to care.

"So, what were you saying about our parents?" Kale asked.

"Well, I was due to land on Howland Island, but there was a little glitch in the navigational system, so I ended up having to land on Gilly Guns Island instead."

"Wait," said Jaundice, looking at her sister. "We've been there."

Kale nodded. Not too long ago, an evil pirate queen had marooned the Bland Sisters on Gilly Guns Island, if only temporarily.

"So you know how spectacular it is," Beatrix said. She sighed. "I could have stayed there forever, exploring and researching the flora and fauna. But then I ran into your parents, and we all escaped together, with the help of one of

CAPTAIN ANN TENNILLE

their friends . . . she was named Captain Ann something—"

"Captain Ann Tennille!" Kale said, remembering the heroic privateer who had rescued them, too.

"That's the one," said Beatrix, buttering her corn muffin.

"Did our parents say where they were going?" asked Jaundice.

"Your mother said she needed to confront an old nemesis," said Beatrix. "She and your father talked about you two, and how they couldn't wait to see you again."

The Bland Sisters put their hands over their hearts and looked at each other. There was that ache again. Kale closed her eyes, as the memories came flooding back.

She remembered a moment when her father had taken her and her sister outside their house and sat them on a blanket in the grass while he did some yard work. She'd been crying about some particularly bright flowers, and so he'd shielded her eyes and brought her back inside. His hand, she recalled, smelled like the lavender he'd been pruning. The scent was overwhelming to her then, but she remembered it now with a certain fondness.

"You two should be glad you have parents who encourage you to explore the world," Beatrix said. "Mine stopped talking to me when I took up flying."

"They don't talk to you, at all?" Kale asked. At least the Bland Sisters' parents sent them letters, and talked to them in their dreams.

"They didn't even like it when I was just a journalist. Though when someone finally hired me as a reporter, they only wanted me writing puff pieces. You know: what's the latest fashion, how are women wearing their hair these days, what's the best place to get married, et cetera, ad nauseam. I wanted to write about serious things, *real news*. And then my boss had an idea: I would fly around the world."

"That sounds exciting," said Kale. The mere mention of flying gave Jaundice a small wave of nausea. She put down her spoonful of oatmeal.

"Well, there was one catch: I wouldn't be doing the flying. They just wanted me to write about being a *passenger* on this new luxury plane. They had a photographer onboard to take pictures of me wearing different outfits. I felt like a doll, not a journalist. The only good part of it was that I got to travel to so many different places. Once I got home, I knew I just had to go out and see the world again. But on my own terms. So, I quit my job and signed up for flying lessons. My parents think that flying is dangerous."

"But it's not?" asked Kale.

"No, it is," said Beatrix, spearing some pancakes and sausage with her fork. "That's why I like it! Life's not worth living unless we're taking risks and challenging ourselves. Don't you think?"

The Bland Sisters considered this. If one took too many risks, wasn't one in danger of not being alive at all?

"I left everything behind to pursue my aviation training abroad—no one would teach me back home," said Beatrix.

"Why not?" asked Jaundice.

"Because of the color of my skin," Beatrix informed them.

Jaundice and Kale looked at each other, then at the pilot. Beatrix put down her fork.

"You do know what *prejudice* is, don't you?" she asked.

Kale thought for a moment. "It's hostile or unfair thinking or behavior, based on untrue ideas," she said.

"That's what it said in *Dr. Nathaniel Snoote's Illustrated Children's Dictionary*, may he rest in pieces." Not long ago, the Bland Sisters had lost their beloved dictionary, but they would never forget its helpful definitions.

"Well, reading about something and experiencing it in real life, all your life, are two different things," Beatrix said.

"By staying at home all those years, we missed out on quite a bit," Kale noted. "Not all of it good."

"We still have a lot to learn," Jaundice said.

"Clearly," said Beatrix, raising an eyebrow. "I've spent my life flying around the world, learning everything there is to know about it, good and bad. Now, I'm on a special assignment for the Egyptian Antiquities Service. I'm supposed to fly over the Valley of the Kings in Luxor and look for illegal digging sites. That's how I met up with your parents again."

"What does that have to do with our parents?" Jaundice asked.

Beatrix looked at them both. "You don't know? About your mother?" she asked.

Jaundice and Kale shook their heads.

"Your mother was born in Cairo—she studied archaeology there," Beatrix explained. "And she worked on sites in the Valley of the Kings."

"Archaeology is the study of history, through excavation and analysis," Kale said to Jaundice.

"And excavation means digging," Jaundice replied. "I wonder if that's what our mother was doing in my dream."

"Wait," said Kale. "If our mother was born in Cairo, does that mean we're . . . Egyptian?"

"Half Egyptian," Beatrix said, looking the Bland Sisters up and down. "Though you two look a *lot* more like your father."

"All this time, we thought we were one-hundred-percent from Dullsville," Jaundice said.

"But it turns out there's another part of the world that's a part of *us*, too," said Kale.

"Hattie and Bert met in Egypt, I think," Beatrix explained.

"Hattie," said Jaundice.

"And Bert," said Kale. The Bland Sisters had never heard their parents' real names before; they'd always known them by what they now knew to be their aliases, John and Mary Bland, or rather, Mother and Father. Jaundice and Kale closed their eyes and bowed their heads. Just feeling the words on their tongues filled them with longing.

"Right," Beatrix said slowly. "How long has it been since you've seen them?"

The Bland Sisters looked at each other and shrugged. They couldn't remember. Their parents had left them to run an errand of an unspecified nature so very long ago. Since then, Jaundice and Kale had been on their own.

"Well, I'm sure they can't wait to see you," said the pilot. "And to know you're safe."

She reached into her coat and pulled out a worn little book.

"I got a package yesterday from your parents. It contained the coordinates to your house, a quick note about rendezvousing with us at a secret spot—to be named later—and this. Does it look familiar?" Beatrix asked.

The black cover of the book was sun-faded, and the pages inside were filled with notes, sketches, maps, and diagrams, all written in brown ink in a familiar hand.

"That's the handwriting on all our letters," Jaundice said, leafing through it. The fact that the book seemed gray on the outside and brown on the inside was comforting, given that those were Jaundice and Kale's favorite colors, respectively. She handed it to Kale, who gave it a good sniff.

"Mmm," she said, closing her eyes. "Spices."

"This is your mother's archaeology journal—she started it when she was a student. She showed it to me on Gilly Guns Island, and told me how she takes it with her everywhere," explained the pilot. "So the fact that she sent it to me has only one meaning: Danger."

"For us, or for our parents?"

"Both," said Beatrix. "Luckily, 'Danger' is my middle name."

"Really?" said Kale.

"No, it's Louise, after my grandmother," the pilot confessed. "But don't worry, ladies. You're in good hands."

"I heard someone ordered the Barnstormer," a woman said, appearing at their table. "There's only one person I know who can handle all that food."

"Ricky!" Beatrix said, jumping up to embrace the woman. They looked into each other's eyes, smiling. "It's been a while."

"Too long," Ricky said. She looked over at the Bland Sisters. "And who are these ladies?"

"My precious cargo," Beatrix explained. "Ricky, this is Jaundice and Kale Bland. Jaundice and Kale, this is Ricky. She owns the whole kit and caboodle here. She and I got into quite a bit of trouble together when we were younger."

"Time does go by," Ricky said, sighing.

"Well, we'll always have Paris," Beatrix noted.

"That's true," Ricky said. "And here she is now!"

At that, the café owner picked something up from the

floor and held it aloft for the Bland Sisters to see. It was a
large and very old-looking tortoise with a bumpy brown shell.

"We rescued her in France on one of our last adventures
together," explained Beatrix.

"Say hello to Paris, girls," Ricky urged.

"Hello, Paris," Jaundice and Kale said. The tortoise
promptly retreated into its shell.

"How long are you here?" Ricky asked.

"As long as it takes to fill my belly," said Beatrix.

"Not long, then," Ricky said, giving Jaundice and Kale
a wink. "I've never seen someone eat so much, so fast. She
might even eat faster than she flies—that's why we named
the Barnstormer after her. Wait. Did you say your names are
Jaundice and Kale?"

"We didn't," said Jaundice.

"But we are," said Kale.

"I've seen those names before," Ricky said. She closed her eyes for a moment. "Where was it?"

Somewhere in the kitchen, a radio was turned on. A dreamy song filled the air.

Ricky sighed. "Ugh," she said. "I've told my cook a million times, I can't think with that sad music dripping in my ears."

"You were never the sentimental type," recalled Beatrix.

"I'm sure it will come to me," Ricky said. She headed back to the kitchen and shouted at the cook, "I told you not to play it again, Sam!"

While Beatrix and the Bland Sisters continued eating, the big-eyed man in the hat paid his bill, rose from his seat, and began walking to the door. Thankfully, Jaundice had just paused to blow on her spoonful of still-warm oatmeal, or she would not have noticed that the man was stealing Kale's backpack.

"Stop! Thief!" she yelled.

"Oh, no!" Kale shouted. "He's making off with *TAKING OFF! with Trip Winger!*"

Beatrix was up in a flash. She tripped the man, and he landed on the floor, dropping the backpack. But just as Beatrix reached down to grab it, the man reached up and

pulled her down, too. For a few moments, they tussled. Then they both sprang up and began fighting.

"She's awfully good with her fists," noted Kale.

"Unfortunately, so is he," said Jaundice.

Finally, the man kicked one of the café chairs at Beatrix. She stumbled out of the way, which gave him just enough time to grab the backpack and run. He was headed for the door, when—

BONGGGGG.

He ran right into a frying pan—a pan wielded by Ricky, standing in the kitchen doorway.

"Four things you won't find in my café: rats, roaches, sad music, and thieves," she announced. The Bland Sisters took note.

TO BANK (OR TURN) THE PLANE SMOOTHLY, MOVE THE
STICK TO THE LEFT OR RIGHT. KEEP AN EYE ON YOUR
TURN–AND–BANK INDICATOR AND ADJUST THE RUDDER
ACCORDINGLY TO KEEP THE BALL IN THE CENTER.

TAKING OFF! with Trip Winger

Chapter Three

B eatrix grabbed a pitcher of ice water and threw it in the man's face. He regained consciousness, sputtering and flailing.

"Who are you?" she asked him, grabbing him by the collar.

"I . . . I am Uggo," the man said, finally. "Please. My master only sent me to retrieve what is rightfully his."

"Who is your master?" Beatrix asked. When the man said nothing, she gave him a good shake.

Filled with fear, his eyes looked even more bug-like. When he opened his mouth to speak, nothing came out. Finally, he raised his hand, and extended two shaky fingers.

"Two?" said Jaundice. "What does that mean?"

"It's not 'two,'" Beatrix said. She let Uggo go, and he slumped to the floor, moaning. "It's the letter V."

"What does that mean?" asked Kale, collecting her backpack.

"It means we need to get going, pronto," said Beatrix.

"What do you want me to do with this trash?" asked Ricky, nudging Uggo with her boot. "Shall I alert the authorities?"

"No, I think we should send him back to his 'master,'" Beatrix decided. She knelt down and addressed Uggo. "You tell 'V' that if he wants it, he's got to go through me. And I can't *wait* for him to try."

The pilot downed her glass of orange juice.

"We've gotta go, ladies," Beatrix announced.

"Where?" asked Jaundice.

"I don't know yet," said Beatrix. "Anywhere but here."

As the Bland Sisters and the pilot made their way back to the Bluebird, Ricky ran after them.

"Wait! I finally remembered!" she cried, waving a worn postcard. She handed it to Kale. "This came for you yesterday."

Kale gave it a good sniff. She handed it to Jaundice, who sniffed it, too.

"It's from our parents," the Bland Sisters said in unison.

"They told me they'd send word of where we should rendezvous," Beatrix informed them. "What does it say?"

"Nothing," said Jaundice. One side featured a photo of a camel and said GREETINGS FROM LUXOR. WISH YOU WERE HERE. She flipped the postcard over. "The other side is just doodles."

"Let me see that," said Beatrix, taking a look for herself. She chuckled. "These aren't doodles. It's a hieroglyph."

"Is that like a code?" asked Kale.

"It is," said Beatrix. "It's an ancient written language made of pictures. In this case, this sequence of pictures spells out a word."

"What word?" asked Jaundice, peering over the pilot's shoulder.

"It's *QAD*. It's the ancient Egyptian word for 'sleep,'" said Beatrix.

Ricky shrugged. "I don't get it," she said. "How is 'sleep' going to help you find them?"

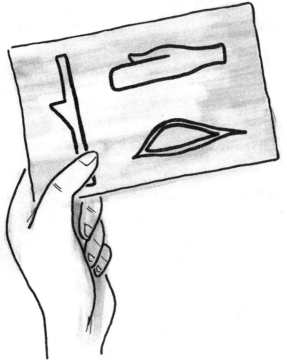

"Oh, wait," Kale said, turning to her sister. "Maybe we're supposed to sleep with the scarab under our pillow. Then we can talk to our parents, and they can tell us where they are."

But Jaundice wasn't listening. Her eyes were squeezed shut, as if she was thinking really, really hard.

"Sister?" said Kale.

"I think they already told us where they are," Jaundice said. "Remember that dream I had on the plane?"

"That dream didn't make any sense," Kale reminded her.

"Tell me everything you saw," Beatrix said.

"Well, at first, it was snowing, and really cold," said Jaundice. "And there was this really fancy castle. I went inside, and then I was outside again, but it was warm and sunny, and there were flowers and plants everywhere. Our parents were there, and our mother was poking around in the dirt with strange tools. There was a boy and a girl there, in white robes, and they wanted me to give them the scarab. And then I woke up."

"Yep," said Kale. "Complete nonsense."

Beatrix squinted. "Hmm," she said. "It might not be. Not completely, anyway. When you put snow together with a fancy castle, there's only one place that comes to mind in Luxor: the Winter Palace."

"'The Winter Palace'? Sounds cold," said Kale.

"It isn't. Believe me," said Beatrix.

"You'll need provisions," said Ricky. She ran back to the souvenir shop in the terminal and returned with hats and sunglasses and water canteens and a big bottle of sunscreen. "If there's one thing I learned on my travels, it's that the sun is not your friend!"

The Bland Sisters took the items from Ricky eagerly. They had never been on friendly terms with the sun, so they appreciated the extra protection.

"Now we'd better take to the skies," said Beatrix, donning her goggles and preparing the Bluebird for takeoff.

"I guess this is goodbye," said Ricky.

"Goodbye!" called the Bland Sisters, stepping onto the plane.

"Thanks for the oatmeal!" said Jaundice. "And the provisions!"

"And for that thing you did with the frying pan!" called Kale.

"Here's looking at you, kid!" said Beatrix, blowing Ricky a kiss.

• • •

Beatrix showed Kale how all of the dials and levers and pedals worked in the cockpit. She even allowed Kale to help her fly the plane a little bit, and she showed her how to lower and retract the Bluebird's amphibious landing gear.

"Will we be landing on . . . water?" Kale asked.

"Just a little river," said Beatrix. "Nothing we can't handle."

"I'm having a Feeling," Kale announced, as she gripped the steering column. Kale was always having Feelings of one kind or another, but this Feeling was one she could not describe. It made the hair on the back of her neck stand up. It gave her goosebumps.

"I think you're a natural," Beatrix said. "I wish your parents could see you."

"Me, too," Kale said. "Sister, I'm actually flying the plane!"

"Uuuuuugh," groaned Jaundice. From the moment they'd resumed their seats, she'd been curled up, and sweaty, and green with nausea.

"I wish you'd look outside," Kale called to her. "The landscape below is so perfectly tan." Kale's favorite color was brown, so she may have been slightly biased.

"That's sand," Beatrix informed her. "We're flying over the desert."

"I can't look," said Jaundice. She squeezed her eyes shut even more tightly.

"I think your sister might be suffering from a fear of
flying, otherwise known as aviophobia," Beatrix surmised.
"Of course, she might just have acrophobia, which is a fear of
heights, or claustrophobia, which is a fear of being confined.
I decided to learn all I could about fear at an early age, so I'd
know what to do if I ever felt afraid."

"And have you?" Kale asked. "Felt afraid?"

"Oh, all the time," Beatrix said. "That's when I know things are really getting exciting. I find the best way to deal with fear is to confront it head-on."

"Blerrrrrgh," Jaundice moaned. She was about to have a head-on confrontation with her breakfast.

Kale left the cockpit and sat next to her sister. "Why don't I read to you from our mother's journal? I'm sure hearing her words will comfort both of us."

Jaundice groaned in response. Kale took this as a sign to commence reading.

PROPERTY OF HATSHEPSUT UMM
Student of Archaeology
DAY ONE: THE JOB (!!!)

I can't believe it — I'm going to be assisting my idol, the world-renowned archaeologist and Egyptologist, Victor Gazebo!

There were dozens of other applicants, all of whom were just as qualified as me, so I never thought I had a chance. But then I got the call, inviting me to Professor Gazebo's office for an interview. I'd never seen so many books on ancient Egypt in one place, or so many artifacts (he assured me they were reproductions), and Professor Gazebo is even more intimidating in person. I couldn't believe I was in the same room with him, let alone interviewing for a job as his assistant.

He asked me a few questions about my education and background, and I told him all about my work at the university. He didn't seem impressed, especially when he noticed my snake bracelet.

"I am not a fan of snakes, Miss Umm," he informed me, frowning. "In any form."

I covered the bracelet with my hand. Of course, I thought I was sunk. But then he looked at my resume.

"Your first name is . . . Hatshepsut?" he said.

"It is," I replied. "Hatshepsut Umm. Though everyone calls me Hattie."

"You are named after the great Egyptian queen?" he said.

"That's right," I said. "My parents always had high hopes for me. I only wish they'd lived long enough for me to fulfill them."

He folded his hands and looked at me, his eyes glittering.

"Miss Umm," he said. "I cannot say that you are any more qualified than any of the other applicants for this position. But I can tell you that I am a believer in signs. The work I am finishing up right now is focused on the Temple of Amon in Karnak. A pair of obelisks was erected in front of that temple, though only one still stands. They were built by—"

"Queen Hatshepsut," I said.

He leaned forward and focused his piercing eyes on me.

"Are you a hard worker, Miss Umm? Can you promise to be obedient, loyal, and above all, discreet?"

"I will do whatever you ask," I said.

"Welcome to my team," he said, making a V sign with his fingers.

Victor, Temple of Amon

DAY FIFTEEN

We've been working on finishing the Temple of Amon project for the past two weeks. It's been the hardest work I've ever done. Most of the time I follow Victor around, making notes and attending to his lunch orders and making sure he always has his perfectly-ice-cold qasab and his afternoon nap (I've even shared my mother's sleep method to cure his insomnia). And then, today, everything changed.

    I was at the café, buying Victor's lunch of fattoush and

qasab (he will only eat the fattoush there, since they make it with kale, which is evidently healthier) when I saw a young man at the bar. I could tell by his clothes that he was a tourist, though for someone here on holiday, he seemed particularly unhappy. I don't know what made me do it, but I ordered an extra qasab and set it in front of him.

"Have a nice day," I said to him in English, hoping it was a language he could understand. Before he could respond, I left.

Why did I do it? I don't know. Perhaps it's because of all the good work I've been doing with Victor. It inspired me to do a good deed.

When I got back to the site with Victor's lunch, he was in an uncharacteristically happy mood. He was laughing and joking with the members of his security detail, who guard his dig sites from looters (and make sure to dispense with any errant snakes). He even remembered to pay me for his lunch without having to remind him.

"This is a day for the history books," he said, taking a swig of qasab. "My workmen on the new site have broken through!"

"Broken through?" I asked.

He showed me a map unrolled on his desk.

"This is the tomb of Seti I," I said. "It was discovered by Giovanni Battista Belzoni in 1817."

"Correct. And since then, it has been 'fully excavated.'

FIG 1: Glasses of Qasab at café

Until now," he said, smirking. "Tell me, who inherited the throne from Seti I?"

I thought for a moment. "His son, Ramses II?"

"Eventually," said Victor. "Through my research, I have learned that Ramses was not the first in line. Seti I had two other children. Twins—a boy and a girl. Their names were Nehy and Nefret."

"What happened to them?" I asked.

"They succumbed to influenza when they were children,"

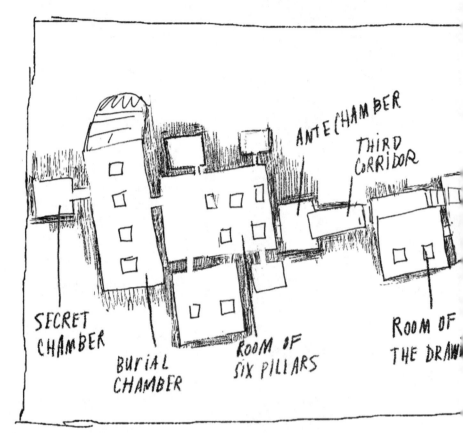

SECRET CHAMBER

BURIAL CHAMBER

ROOM OF SIX PILLARS

ANTECHAMBER

THIRD CORRIDOR

ROOM OF THE DRAW

Victor informed me. "For some time, I have suspected that they were buried in a secret chamber in Seti's tomb. I believe my team has just found that chamber. We go there tomorrow."

"What about our work here, at the temple?" I asked.

"Our work here is done," he said. He sat down and unwrapped his fattoush. He took a big bite of kale. "Our real work is just beginning!"

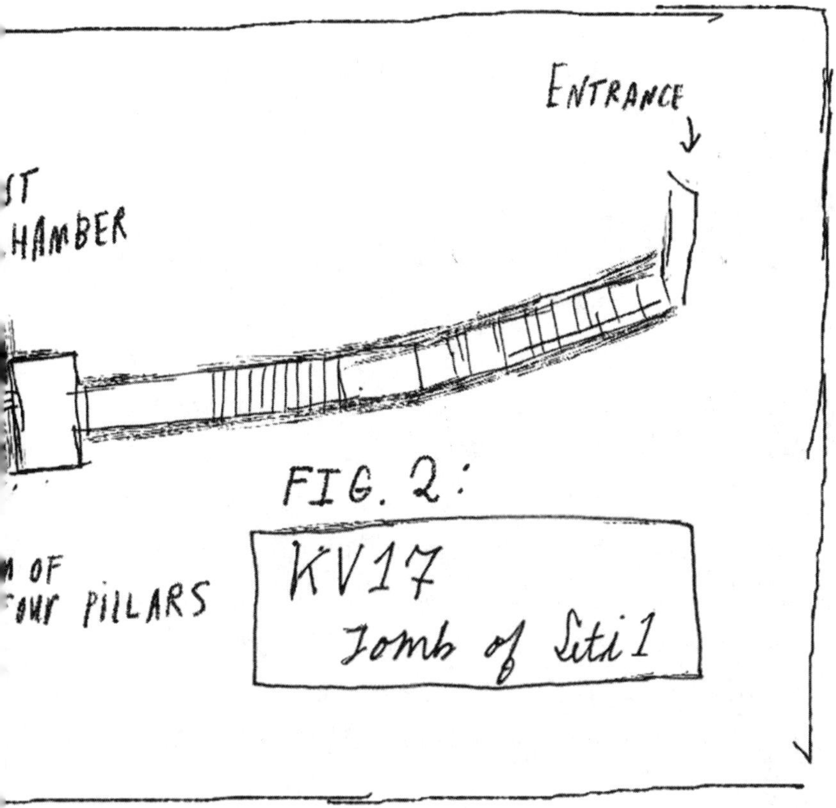

FIG. 2:

KV17
Tomb of Seti 1

ST
HAMBER

OF
our PILLARS

ENTRANCE

DAY TWENTY-FIVE

We've been working in the secret burial chamber of Nehy and Nefret (Victor calls it "Project N") for about a week now. As ever, the work is slow. All manner of artifacts have been uncovered, including musical instruments, pieces of pottery, statue fragments, jewelry and beads, games, toys, and several dolls. It's as if the playroom of these twins was packed up and re-created in their tomb, for eternity. It's sad, but in a way, kind of nice. And it is satisfying to know that all of the antiquities we've excavated will soon be on display in the Egyptian Museum in Cairo, so we can observe and admire and learn from our past. This is why I became an archaeologist, to share the lessons of history with my country, and the world.

Unfortunately, Victor is not satisfied, as the playroom has not revealed his most sought-after treasure: a pair of scarabs, made specially for Nehy and Nefret.

"According to my research, they were created by one of the greatest craftsmen in all of ancient Egypt—a man named Huya," Victor explained. "It was said that the gods bestowed him with special powers, and that he used those powers in his work. When placed beneath the children's heads, the scarabs allowed them to communicate with each other in their dreams."

"So, you believe in this myth, about the scarabs' magic?" I asked.

"I prefer to leave my mind open to any and all possibilities, Miss Umm," he informed me. I resolved to do the same.

Aside from the security detail, the rest of the staff was dismissed tonight, and I was hoping to get ahead on itemizing the day's discoveries. I was crouched behind an assemblage of shabti figurines when Victor came in. I could tell he didn't know I was there, but for some reason, I didn't move or make any noise; I just waited and watched. That's when I saw him pick up one of the dolls and put it in his jacket pocket.

Finally, I revealed myself. "What are you doing with that doll?" I asked.

At first, Victor seemed surprised to see me there, then he laughed and patted his pocket.

"Bringing her back to my office," he explained. "This one deserves closer examination."

"I'm sorry," I said. "I didn't mean —"

"It's all right, Miss Umm. You have an inquisitive mind. That's one of the reasons I hired you," Victor said.

"Thank you, sir. I appreciate that," I said.

"Just remember what they say about curiosity," Victor said, smiling. At this, he pointed at a mummified cat.

Writing about it now, I feel so silly. Did I really think that my mentor was trying to steal one of his own discoveries? Next time, think before you speak, Hattie!

P.S. The name of the young man at the café is Albertus Magnus Jr., but he prefers that I call him Bert. I see him every afternoon now, when I arrive for Victor's lunch order. He has a very unassuming way about him, though I do like his sense of humor, and the way he really seems to listen to me. And I like his traveling vest, which seems to have an infinite number of pockets —he's always pulling one thing or another from them, like a handkerchief when I sneeze, or an umbrella when it's raining, or a handful of the date candy I like.

It turns out Bert is from a place called Dullsville, which doesn't sound very promising, but he tells me he comes from a long line of magicians.

"That's funny," I said when he told me. "You don't look like a magician."

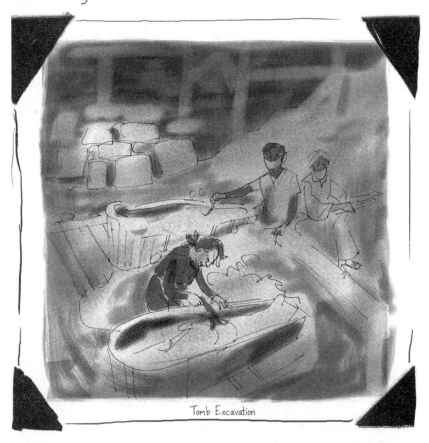

Tomb Excavation

"That's because I'm not," he said. "My father, Albertus Magnus Sr., wanted me to become a magician, too. But my heart just wasn't in it. So he threw me out of the house. I've been traveling all over the world since then, trying to find my purpose."

"And have you?" I asked.

Bert took my hand.

"I think so," he said, smiling.

DAY THIRTY-FIVE

Finally, we have catalogued all of the artifacts in the chamber—well, not all of them. We saved the best for last—the sarcophagi of Nehy and Nefret, the Lost Twins of Seti I.

I have never been present at the opening of an ancient Egyptian stone coffin; it is, as one might imagine, a sensitive and time-consuming process, ultimately involving quite a few ropes and pulleys and heave-ho. But eventually, the lid was lifted. Inside the alabaster outer box was the beautifully wrapped mummy of Nehy, son of Seti I and twin brother of Nefret. Unfortunately, we could not remove the gold-painted shroud covering his face, but Victor found something remarkable hidden in the wrappings behind the mummy's head: one of the legendary scarabs.

I held it in my hand for just a moment. It was green and intricately carved, and surprisingly warm. Within a few moments, Victor took it back from me.

"The value of this is incomprehensible," he muttered.

"To the museum, you mean," I said. "And to Egypt."

"Of course," Victor said, sniffing. "But we'll need both of them. We'll only know if they work when we have the set. Then we'll really be in business. When we open Nefret's sarcophagus tomorrow, I can only hope we'll find the other scarab."

Everyone has gone off to celebrate, and I am just about to wrap things up here. One way or another, tomorrow will be a big day for Project N!

FIG. 3:

Scarabs

DAY THIRTY-SIX

Well, I was right. It's been a big day for Project N, but not in any way I could have imagined. It all started last night.

I went to deliver Victor's mail to his office, but the door was locked. Fortunately, I know where he keeps the key: behind the statue of Sekhmet that guards his office door.

When I got inside, the place was a mess—boxes and packing materials were everywhere. I put the mail on his desk, and that's when I saw the clipboard. On it was a list. In one column, it catalogued many of the artifacts unearthed during the Project N dig. In the second column, it listed names and addresses. In the third, it listed numbers. They were large numbers with many zeroes at the end. It dawned on me that they were dollar amounts.

I looked around the room again as it all began to sink in.

I saw musical instruments, pieces of pottery, statue fragments, jewelry and beads, games, toys, and a familiar doll—the one I caught Victor slipping into his pocket that day. Then I saw the scarab we'd just unearthed that morning. He was planning on selling it all!

"I locked this door for a reason," Victor said. He stood in the doorway, his satchel slung over one shoulder. It seemed heavy. I wondered what other stolen treasures it might contain.

"I was just . . . delivering your mail," I explained.

"You are a diligent assistant, Miss Umm," he said, smiling. "Perhaps too diligent."

"That's why you hired me," I reminded him. "You asked me if I was a hard worker."

"And I asked you if you could be obedient, loyal, and above all . . . discreet," he reminded me.

"I have been. And I will be," I said.

49

He took the clipboard from me.

"We have to please our patrons," he explained. "How else do you think we can afford our work? The pittance we receive from the government does not begin to cover what we need."

I looked at Victor's diamond ankh pinkie ring, and at the box of fine cigars on his desk. His shiny new car was probably parked right out front. It's clear that his "needs" are much different than mine.

"Our patrons are very important people. Some are even very dangerous people. There's no telling what they might do if we don't give them what they want," he said. "And most of these things are just trifles, really."

"But the scarabs are special," I said.

"You're right. They are special," he said. "And they will fetch a special price. I already have more than a few interested buyers. As long as we have the set, and we can prove they work, my financial situation should be improving tremendously."

"They are priceless," I argued. "They belong with Nehy and Nefret."

"Nehy and Nefret have been dead for thousands of years. It's time for the living to benefit from the value of these treasures," Victor said.

"You are an archaeologist. An Egyptologist. It's your job to preserve these antiquities for the people of Egypt, not sell them off to the highest bidder!" I said.

"Just think of the work we could do together with that kind of money," Victor said.

"Together?" I said.

"I've been thinking about promoting you for some time now," he said. "Your intellect and your potential are more than clear. But I'd need to know that you're truly ready to invest in our work. OUR work, Hattie. We could be . . . partners."

"I don't know what to say," I said.

"Say yes," Victor said. "When everyone does what they're told, everyone wins. Believe me."

Something in his tone of voice scared me—and made me realize I should just play along.

"Then, yes," I said. "I accept."

"Good girl," he said. Victor put his hands on my shoulders. His fingers squeezed a little too hard as he looked into my eyes.

"If I didn't think I could trust you, it would be a shame," he said. "For you."

I was so shaken after my meeting with Victor, I could barely dial my phone to call Bert. We met at the café that night, and I told him everything.

"You need to turn him in," he said. "He's nothing but a rotten thief!"

"If I turn him in, there's no telling what might happen to me," I said. "Victor made that painfully clear."

Bert finished his drink. He looked at me.

"You should just run away, then," he said. "That's what I did, when my father threw me out."

I laughed. "You can't be serious," I said.

"I'm almost always serious," he said.

"I'm not going to leave my life here," I said. "Besides, where would I go?"

"Anywhere. Everywhere," Bert said.

The thought did sound enticing. I've never been anywhere other than Egypt. All my life, I've dreamed of exploring other lands and discovering other cultures.

"But my work is here," I reminded him.

"As long as you're working for Victor Gazebo, you'll never be free," said Bert.

I stared down at my own empty glass. I knew he was right.

I left Bert and went straight to the police station, determined to do the right thing and tell the authorities everything I knew. When I got there, several uniformed officers were on duty. I was about to approach one of them when I realized he looked familiar. In fact, more than a few of them looked familiar—they'd been part of Victor's security detail, the ones he'd laughed and joked with. One of them made eye contact with me; he smiled and made the V sign with his fingers. I made one in return, then hurried out.

As I rushed home, I thought about what Bert said. As long as I work for Victor, I will never be free. Maybe I could just quit, and find another archaeology job somewhere else. I could promise Victor I'd never reveal his scheme. But then I'd have to watch him sell off those priceless treasures, like the scarabs, and deny the people of Egypt their legacy. I couldn't live with myself.

I was just about to turn the corner onto my street when I saw him: another one of the members of Victor's security detail, standing across the street from my apartment. He kept looking over at the door to my building and arguing with someone on his walkie-talkie.

In my surprise, I let out a little cry. He turned his head, and our eyes met.

And then I began to run.

Thankfully, he didn't seem to know the streets of my neighborhood as well as I do, because I was able to duck into an alley and evade him. I waited a few minutes to make sure the coast was clear, and then I called Bert. He told me where he was staying, at the Winter Palace. By the time I got there, I'd made up my mind.

"I am going to run away," I said. "If I don't, there's no telling what might happen to me."

Bert picked up a suitcase. "I had a feeling you might say that," he said. "I've already packed."

"Why?" I said.

"Because I'm coming with you," he said.

"Why?" I said.

"Because I love you," he said.

I blinked.

"I love you, too," I said.

Bert took my hand.

"Then let's do it," he said.

"There's something I have to do first," I said. "I'll meet you at the airport in an hour."

"I'll buy the tickets," he said.

"You'll have to change our names," I said.

"Why?" he asked.

"Because what I'm about to do is going to make Victor very, very angry."

I left Bert and went back to Victor's office, where I unlocked the door again and crept inside. The clipboard I'd hoped to take, which held Victor's list of buyers, was gone. I panicked . . . and then I saw the scarab. I held it in my hand again, feeling its warmth.

"Someday, I will find your twin, Nehy," I said. "I will wait until Victor has his guard down. If it takes my whole life, I will reunite you and Nefret."

I put the scarab in my pocket.

I might not be able to expose his illegal scheme, but as long as I have one scarab, I know Victor can never sell them as a set. I know that as long as I have it, he will always be searching for it, and me. But I also know it's a risk I have to take.

Bert was waiting for me at the airport. When I saw him sitting at the gate, I realized I didn't have anything but my satchel, containing the scarab and my journal. Everything else I owned was back at my apartment. But I couldn't go back. Ever.

"I was worried you weren't going to show up," he said. "Our plane is just about to board."

"Where are we going?" I asked. I thought about my mother, who wanted me to stay close to home after my father died. Now that she's gone, too, I have no family, no one who cares where I go or what I do.

"First stop: Peru. I have friends all over the world now. I can't wait for them to meet you," he said. "And if we really need to disappear, we can go to Dullsville, the town where I grew up. Believe me, Gazebo will never find us there," he said.

Maybe I've made a big mistake, I thought. I should never have taken the scarab. I should never have brought Bert into this.

"I changed our names, just like you asked. We're now 'John and Mary Bland,'" he said. He took a little box out of one of his vest pockets and opened it up. Inside was a silver

55

ring. "And I bought this at the bazaar. It's all I could get, for now. But I figure if we're going to spend the foreseeable future running from danger together, we may as well make it official. Will you marry me, Hattie—I mean, Mary?"

I looked at the ring, and at Bert. Could we make a life together, always looking over our shoulders, waiting for Victor to exact his revenge?

"Is everything all right?" he said.

I nodded. I slipped the ring on my finger. Then I took his hand.

"Let's go," I said.

FIG. 4:
One of the two
obelisks of Hatshepsut

Chapter Four

It's incredible," Kale said, after reading about Hattie and Bert's daring escape from Luxor. "I really felt as if I was right there with them. Didn't you?"

Jaundice nodded. Though her eyes were still shut, and her skin was still clammy and vaguely green, Kale's narration of the events was a comfort. "Is there more?" she managed.

Kale flipped through the remaining pages. Most of them were blank, until the very end of the journal. On the inside cover, two little envelopes were taped to the page, along with what looked like a ticket.

"One of the envelopes is labeled, *Kale, for the salad that brought us together.* The other is labeled, *Jaundice, for the symptom of the malaria that almost killed us on our second honeymoon to Madagascar.*"

Kale opened the envelopes. Inside each was a tiny lock of hair in an all-too-familiar brown shade.

"I guess that explains how they named us," she said.

Then she read the fine print on the envelopes.

"Jaundice?" Kale said.

"Mmm?" Jaundice moaned.

"These numbers on the envelopes look like birth dates," Kale said.

"Well, that's handy," said Jaundice. "We'll finally know when to celebrate."

Up to now, the Bland Sisters couldn't remember when their birthdays were, and had no parents to tell them, so they decided it might as well be February 29, Leap Day. That way they'd only need to worry about it once every four years.

"Right," said Kale. "Well, the good news is that our birthdays aren't on Leap Day."

"What's the bad news?" asked Jaundice.

"Our birthdays . . . aren't on the same day. They're not even in the same *year*," said Kale, rubbing her temples. Anything but the simplest mathematics gave her a headache.

"What do you mean?" asked Jaundice, opening one eye so she could see for herself.

But there it was.

One envelope read, *KALE BLAND, born December 31, 11:58* P.M.

The other read, *JAUNDICE BLAND, born January 1, 12:15* A.M.

"So I'm seventeen minutes younger than you, but because I was born after midnight, my birthday's a whole year later?" said Jaundice. She was very good at numbers, even through her aviophobic nausea.

"I can't believe it," said Kale, shaking her head. "I always thought we'd have the same birthday, like real twins."

"I always thought I was born first," Jaundice admitted.

"We're just outside Luxor," Beatrix announced from the cockpit. "Does anyone back there want to help me land this thing?"

"Oh, me-me-me!" said Kale, waving her hand. She was surprised by her own enthusiasm—but then, she remembered, she *was* the older sister. Perhaps she was supposed to be more take-charge.

"Landing on water can be tricky, but I know you can do it," Beatrix said. "There's nothing like being on the Nile."

"Did you say 'in denial'?" Kale asked. "Because I've definitely been *there* before."

Helped by Beatrix, Kale managed to land the plane on the river with relatively little turbulence. Beatrix also taught her how to drain the plane's hull and raise its amphibious gear when it was time for takeoff.

"You're on your way to being a superlative pilot. You just need more practice," Beatrix informed her, as everything in the cockpit and cabin finally settled—including Jaundice. And when Beatrix and Kale taxied the Bluebird to the riverbank, where a ramp was waiting, Jaundice felt better almost immediately.

"This is our mother's home," she said, taking it all in.

"In a way, it's like our home, too," Kale said, squinting. "It's greener than I imagined."

It was green in Luxor. And brutally hot. Immediately, the Bland Sisters slathered on their sunscreen and donned their hats and sunglasses and canteens.

At the top of the ramp, a man about Beatrix's age seemed to be waiting for them. He was very tall and thin, and like Beatrix, he had very brown skin and an open, kind face. He was wearing a natty suit and a tiny red cap topped with a gold tassel.

"Impeccable timing, O," Beatrix noted, giving the man a hug. "Not much has changed with you, I see."

"Nor with you," said the man.

"Ladies, may I introduce you to my friend, Omar?"

Omar bowed to them.

"I'm Jaundice," said Jaundice.

"And I'm Kale," said Kale.

"These are the Bland Sisters—'John' and 'Mary's' children," Beatrix informed him, giving him a wink.

Omar's eyes grew wide. Then he smiled.

"Please," he said. "Call me 'O.' All my friends do. And the

children of 'John' and 'Mary' are automatically good friends of mine."

"Omar!" a man shouted from one of the barges along the riverbank. Omar waved.

"Ladies, this is my cousin, Ahmed. He works for me," he explained.

"If you need to get across the Nile, anytime, day or night, Omar Excursions is at your service!" called Ahmed.

"Duly noted," said Beatrix. "So you own your own business now?"

Omar handed her a card.

"Well, that seems like a good career move for you," Beatrix said. As they ascended the stairs to the street, she turned to the Bland Sisters. "O knows how to get everywhere. And anything."

"Anything you need in Egypt, I am your man," Omar said.

"We need to get to the Winter Palace," Beatrix announced.

"Fancy," said Omar.

"Yes, fancy. And fast," Beatrix added, grabbing Jaundice's and Kale's hands. "Let's go."

As Omar and Beatrix navigated the tourist crowds, it was all the Bland Sisters could do to hold on. Jaundice was barely fazed by the experience.

"As long as my feet are on the ground, I'm happy," she said.

"So many people," observed Kale, looking around.

"So many sights and colors," said Jaundice. "And smells."

Usually, this much stimulation would have proven overwhelming for the Bland Sisters. But Ricky's trusty sunglasses and hats afforded them just the right amount of protection from any perceived harshness.

"I don't suppose you've seen John and Mary lately?" Beatrix asked Omar.

"Not in the last few days," he said. "We met in a café, where I delivered a few special items they asked me to acquire, including rappelling gear and a blowtorch."

"That sounds . . . like them," said Beatrix.

"From what I hear on the street, they broke into Victor Gazebo's house while he was away and took something from his safe," Omar said.

"I bet that 'something' was the other scarab," said Jaundice. Kale nodded.

"Word is that Victor has placed a bounty on their heads for their capture, for what they stole," Omar added.

"What *they* stole?" Beatrix laughed. "*That's* rich."

"He's nothing but a looter," Omar said, shaking his head.

"A looter?" said Jaundice.

"A thief," explained Beatrix. "There are hundreds of them across this country, hoping to make a quick buck off of antiquities. Most of them are amateurs. Gazebo should know better. He knows how harmful it is to desecrate these landmarks and tombs. He knows that these artifacts don't belong in some rich person's drawing room. They belong in a museum, where everyone can enjoy them."

"Or they belong in their original resting place, where they were meant to be," Omar pointed out. "As the great stories say, if these pharaohs are to have a successful journey into the afterlife, their tombs are to remain undisturbed."

"We're a little too late for that, sadly," said Beatrix. "Ever since Howard Carter unearthed Tut's tomb, it's been a free-for-all around here. These days, antiquities are safer in museums, where their value can be appreciated by anyone and everyone. Admit it, O—you wouldn't have a business if it wasn't for all these tourists."

Omar nodded. "I cannot deny it. But I do try to do my best to educate my customers. My homeland isn't one big souvenir shop."

Even if it wasn't one big souvenir shop, Jaundice and Kale couldn't help noticing that there seemed to be a souvenir shop or stand on just about every corner, selling all manner of artifacts. One even had several tall columns of wrapped rags propped up outside its front door.

"What are those?" asked Kale.

"Mummies," said Beatrix.

Jaundice winced. "What did they ever do to deserve that?" she wondered.

"And what happened to the daddies?" Kale was almost afraid to ask.

"Not 'mommies,'" Beatrix corrected them. "*Mummies.*"

"Ah. Mummies are embalmed bodies," Kale said, recalling the Bland Sisters' helpful dictionary.

"Yes," said Omar. "And it is disgusting how they are displayed, with no respect for the dead."

"We can't be sure those are real," Beatrix said. "There are all sorts of fakers around here."

"Well, we're about to see something very real, and quite spectacular," Omar announced.

The Bland Sisters' mouths fell open. There, facing the majestic Nile, was the largest building either of them had ever seen. It was a beautiful shade of tan, not unlike the sand, Kale thought, and it was wide and tall, with a grand sweeping staircase. At the top of the building were the words WINTER PALACE.

"I thought the Winter Palace would be a castle," said Kale, remembering the illustration next to the definition of *palace* in their dearly-departed dictionary, which featured a majestic castle with towers and turrets and flags.

"It's a hotel," Omar informed them. "The grandest in Egypt."

He led Jaundice and Kale and Beatrix up the stairs and into the lobby, which was no less dramatic. A glittering chandelier tinkled overhead, and a curving marble staircase was flanked by an ornate iron railing.

"Is that you, Howard?" Beatrix asked an older man sitting in the foyer. He wore a three-piece suit and a hat. The man was pale, with a particularly dour expression on his face, but it lightened considerably when he recognized the aviatrix.

"Beatrix," he said, rising from his seat to shake her hand. "Are things still *up in the air* with you?"

"Things are always 'up in the air' with me," she replied.

"I'm actually here with John and Mary's girls. Jaundice, Kale, this is Mr. Carter."

"Pleased to meet you, young ladies," Mr. Carter said, shaking their hands. "Why, you don't look like your mother at all. A shame, really. She's the spitting image of Hatshepsut, one of just a few queens we can confirm reigned as pharaohs. I always hoped to discover her tomb."

"Mr. Carter is a renowned archaeologist," Beatrix explained.

"I was. Now I merely dabble in antiquities," he said. He looked at Beatrix and added, pointedly, "All perfectly legal, mind you."

"Have you seen Mary and John lately, Howard?" Beatrix asked.

"I haven't, sadly," Mr. Carter said. "And you're not the first ones to ask. There were a few women in here earlier today, inquiring after them. Fierce-looking types, all decked out in black leather."

"Sounds like my kind of crowd," said Beatrix, adjusting her own leather jacket.

"Were there six of them?" offered Omar.

Howard Carter nodded. "How did you know?"

"I have heard about them," Omar said. "They are called the Daughters of Sekhmet. A more dangerous bunch you will not find in Luxor."

"Sekhmet was a warrior goddess. Otherwise known as the Mistress of Dread, the Lady of Slaughter, and She Who Mauls," Howard Carter recalled.

"Her followers come from all over the world, to worship and to train," Omar explained. "They enjoy wreaking havoc in her name."

The Bland Sisters' eyes grew wide. They were both considering their usual response to any and all manner of peril: slumping to the floor and pretending to be asleep.

"I bet they're after John and Mary, and that bounty Victor put on their heads," Beatrix said.

"Victor Gazebo, that scoundrel!" Mr. Carter said, grimacing. "He should be in jail for what he's done to Egypt's treasures. Or worse."

"He might be headed there soon, if I have anything to do with it," said Omar.

"We must be going now, Howard," said Beatrix. "You take care."

"You, too," he said. He turned to Jaundice and Kale and tipped his hat. "Good luck, young ladies. If you are anything like your mother, you are destined for greatness."

The Bland Sisters smiled weakly. After hearing about the Daughters of Sekhmet, they could only hope they were destined to survive.

Omar greeted a man behind the reception desk, who was wearing a crisp suit and a bow tie.

"Welcome to the Winter Palace," he said. "I am Mr. Anton. How might I help you?"

"We're looking for our parents," said Jaundice.

"They told us to meet them here," said Kale.

Mr. Anton brought out a large book, with a spine reading REGISTRY in gold. He opened it up and began leafing through it.

"And what are their names?" he asked.

The Bland Sisters looked at each other. Should they give away their parents' true identities? Finally, Beatrix stepped in.

"John and Mary Bland," she informed Mr. Anton. He consulted the book.

"No one here by those names," he said.

"Josephine and Martin Bluth?" the pilot suggested.

Mr. Anton looked again. "No," he said.

"How about Jack and Martha Blergh? Or Jim and Marge Bundt? Or Jeff and Millie Bilge?" asked Beatrix. She looked at the Bland Sisters. "Your parents have accumulated more than a few aliases on their travels."

Again and again, Mr. Anton checked. And again and again, he shook his head.

Beatrix looked around, making sure no one was within earshot. She leaned forward.

"How about . . . Hatshepsut Umm and Albertus Magnus Jr.?" she whispered.

The Bland Sisters put their hands over their hearts. Hearing those names made their hearts ache all over again.

Jaundice remembered a day when their mother was dancing in their kitchen, and singing a song in a language the Bland Sisters did not understand—though Jaundice realized it might have been Egyptian. Their mother had twirled Kale and Jaundice around as she sang and danced, and Jaundice remembered not liking the ensuing dizziness at all. Now, she might be willing to put up with a bit of dizziness—even more than a bit—if it meant being close to their mother again.

"I am sorry," said Mr. Anton. "I see no such listings."

"That can't be," Kale said, raising herself up on tiptoe to get a better look at the ledger. But Mr. Anton closed the book and frowned.

"Perhaps you were misinformed?" he said. "There are many other hotels in Luxor—though of course, none are as fine as the Winter Palace. Best of luck to you in finding your parents."

With that, he turned his attention to the next people in line.

"But, I dreamed it!" Jaundice cried, as Kale pulled her sister away.

"You said our parents told you that not everything in dreams is clear," Kale reminded her. "Maybe we got it wrong."

The Bland Sisters hung their heads. They had come so far. A reunion with their parents had seemed so close at hand.

"Tell me about this dream," said Omar.

Jaundice explained all the details to him, the castle and the snow, and then the field with the flowers and plants. His eyes grew wide.

"Your parents might not be staying here," he said.

The Bland Sisters hung their heads again.

"But I do think they are here," he said. "The field with the flowers and plants, as you describe, sounds much like a garden."

"Of course," said Beatrix.

"And the Winter Palace has the most beautiful garden in all of Luxor. Come, I will show you," Omar said, with a sweep of his arm.

Omar was not kidding. In fact, the scene behind the Winter Palace was spectacular. The gardens contained not just flowerbeds, but vegetable plots, fruit orchards, palm trees, and even tennis and croquet courts.

"It's so . . . colorful," said Jaundice.

"And bright," said Kale. The Bland Sisters put on their sunglasses again, to shield themselves from the glare.

"Well," said Beatrix. "We'd better start searching."

For the next hour, Omar and Beatrix looked everywhere,

Jaundice and Kale trailing behind, trying not to feel too overwhelmed by the bright and varied scenery. Unfortunately, after the hour had transpired, their search party had come up empty-handed.

"Ugh," said Omar. "This is frustrating."

"Not to mention exhausting," said Jaundice, collapsing on a nearby wicker bench. "It certainly looks like they're not here. Though why would they lead us here with all their clues?"

Kale slumped next to her sister. "I'm tired of looking, too," she said. She produced TAKING OFF! *with Trip Winger* from her backpack and started poring over it again. Reading something so dry and practical was always a comfort.

"If you're tired, maybe you *should* sleep," said Beatrix. "In case your parents have another message for you. While you do, Omar and I will keep looking for them."

"And we'll keep our eyes open, in case the Daughters show up," Omar said.

Jaundice reached into her smock pocket, pulled out the scarab, and handed it to Kale.

"Maybe you should try it this time," she suggested. "Since I've already had a turn."

"That's very generous of you," Kale said.

She was right. It was very generous, Jaundice thought. Though she *was* the younger sister, so perhaps she was supposed to be more obliging.

Kale placed the scarab beneath the cushion behind her head.

"Imagine you are floating up, up, up an invisible staircase . . ." she said, repeating her mother's soothing words.

Jaundice yawned. She couldn't help closing her eyes, too.

". . . and into a cozy nest made of feathers and velvet," Kale continued.

It wasn't long before both of the Bland Sisters had fallen asleep.

At first, Kale didn't see her parents. All she saw was sand, and blue sky.

I think I'm in the desert, she thought.

Rising up out of the sand was a roofed structure made of stone. A man with tanned skin and white hair and a pointy nose stood on the front step. He stared down at her menacingly. Then, he spoke.

"Looking for someone?" he said.

"My parents," said Kale.

The man laughed.

"I have what you want, and you have what I want.
Destiny awaits you at the tomb that is larger than large.
Wealth beyond imagining awaits me
with the queen who was a king,
and the twins who are not really twins."

"I don't understand," said Kale. "Is this the dream nonsense Jaundice warned me about?"

A boy and a girl appeared, wearing white robes.

"Nehy and Nefret," Kale whispered.

"The Sacred Scarabs of the Twins are both in use," Nehy said. "When the scarabs are in use, their rightful owners are summoned."

"Return what you have stolen!" Nefret cried. The brother and sister pointed at the man with white hair, and then they pointed at Kale.

"Believe me, we're trying!" Kale said. She turned, and there was her sister, standing next to her. But Jaundice had turned to stone.

"RUN!" a voice shouted. It sounded a lot like Beatrix, though she was nowhere to be seen.

"Run where?" Kale asked.

"We'll meet you by the mummies!" another voice yelled. This one sounded like Omar.

"WAKE UP!" said the Beatrix voice. "The Daughters of Sekhmet are here!"

THE DAUGHTERS OF SEKHMET

❀ ❀ ❀ ❀ ❀ ❀ Chapter Five ❀ ❀ ❀ ❀ ❀ ❀

When the Bland Sisters opened their eyes, they saw
Beatrix and Omar engaged in an all-out melee with
six women wearing black leather jackets and caps. Their eyes
seemed to flicker like flames.

"Did you hear us?" shouted Beatrix.

"We're supposed to run," repeated Kale.

"And meet you by the mummies," repeated Jaundice.

"Good girls," yelled Omar. "Now, get going!"

The Bland Sisters ran as fast as they could in the heat, back
through the lobby of the Winter Palace, where Mr. Carter was

still sitting. He waved to them as they scurried by, out the front door and down the winding staircase to the street.

The bazaar was even busier now, so Jaundice and Kale held hands so as not to get lost in the crowds. The different stands sold all manner of goods—baskets and pots and stone idols and fruits and vegetables and local delicacies. There was even a stand selling scarabs, which Jaundice stopped for a moment to admire.

"We really should go," urged Kale, pulling her sister along. "Do you see the stand with the mummies?"

"It should be just around this corner," said Jaundice. But when they turned the corner, they didn't see any mummies. Instead, they saw one of the Daughters. She was blond and blue-eyed, and she was holding a very large, curved sword, which she looked like she knew how to use. A crowd gathered to watch the "show."

"Surrender to Daughter Betty," the woman informed the Bland Sisters, flashing a lipsticked smile. "Or else."

"What do we do?" Kale asked. "We don't have any weapons."

"Hmm," said Jaundice. She removed her canteen. Quickly, she patted her smock pockets.

Betty tossed her sword from hand to hand, grinning and playing to the crowd. She laughed heartily.

"I guess this is it," said Kale, closing her eyes and grimacing.

"Aha!" said Jaundice, looking down at her canteen. "Yes, it is."

She grabbed the canteen, swung it around her head a few times, and tossed it. It hit Daughter Betty in the head. She fell over backward, knocking over a nearby candy stand.

The crowd cheered. Jaundice merely shrugged.

"Time for a new plan, then," said Kale. She and her sister reversed course, and ended up back in the labyrinth of market stands. One of them was selling rugs.

"I have an idea," said Jaundice. She looked around to make sure the stand's owner wasn't around, and then unrolled a particularly large and ornate rug. "Lie down."

"Lie down?" said Kale. "Shouldn't we be running?"

"That's what they'll *expect*," said Jaundice.

"Ah," said Kale. Jaundice was almost always right.

The Bland Sisters lay down at each end of the rug, then rolled until they were both completely covered and secure inside.

"They'll never find us now," Jaundice said, her voice muffled in the folds of carpet. "We'll just stay here until they go away."

"It's actually quite cozy," said Kale. "If only it weren't so hot. And musty. And I can't seem to find my hat or my sunglasses."

"Shh," said Jaundice.

Within a few moments, they heard a rumbling. Then the rumbling stopped, and they heard whispering. Then it grew quiet.

"I think your idea is working!" said Kale.

"Shh!" said Jaundice.

A few minutes later, the Bland Sisters heard the rumbling again.

"They must be leaving," said Jaundice.

"The sound isn't getting any softer," noted her sister.

The Bland Sisters poked their heads out. They were in the back of a truck with one of the Daughters of Sekhmet. Two more were up front, and the other two were behind the truck on a rumbling motorcycle-with-sidecar.

"What now?" said Kale.

"I don't know," said Jaundice. "I've never been trapped in a rug on a moving truck, surrounded by assassins."

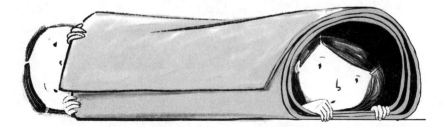

Daughter Fan began arguing with her cohorts in the front of the truck and pointing out the back. Jaundice and Kale were able to wriggle their heads and shoulders out of the rolled-out carpet just enough to see what was going on.

Beatrix was on a horse, galloping toward the truck. She was gaining on them.

"She can ride a horse, too?" said Kale. "Is there nothing she can't do?"

Once Beatrix caught up to Daughter Dot and Daughter Yasmin's motorcycle, she dispensed both with a swift kick and a jackknife wedged in the spokes.

"What a shame," she said, watching the motorcycle and its riders tumble off the road. "My grandmother gave me that knife."

As Beatrix approached the truck, she jumped off the horse and into the back, and was soon engaged in hand-to-hand combat with Daughter Fan. Amidst this impressive display, Daughter Fan flipped around expertly, delivering a kick that left Beatrix groaning in a crumpled heap.

"Oh, no," said Kale.

Daughter Fan smirked, then made the mistake of turning her back. As she did, Beatrix reached out and pulled the assassin's legs out from under her, then swung her off the back of the truck altogether.

"Are you two all right?" she asked the Bland Sisters breathlessly.

"Aside from being surrounded by assassins on a careering truck?" said Kale.

"Well, we need to get you out," said Beatrix, unfurling the rug and freeing them. "I'll be right back. Sit tight."

"We *were* sitting tight. Until you unrolled us," noted Kale. But Beatrix was already making her way to the cab of the truck. With a few swift blows, she subdued Daughter Cosette in the passenger seat.

"Au revoir," said Beatrix, tossing her out.

The one at the wheel, Daughter Ivanka, was a bit more of a challenge. She and Beatrix wrestled with the wheel, making the truck swerve all over the road, nearly colliding with an oncoming car.

"It's funny," Jaundice said. "Being on an airplane for only a moment makes me feel like I'm going to die. But this experience doesn't bother me at all."

"It bothers me a little bit," Kale admitted, her face paler than usual. "Actually, more than a little."

Finally, Beatrix banged Daughter Ivanka's head against the steering wheel and knocked her out. But when she took control of the wheel and looked outside, she realized that the truck was headed for the embankment.

"Jump, girls! Now!" she shouted.

The Bland Sisters did as they were told. Kale was surprised by how much less she enjoyed being airborne without the benefit of being in an airplane, while Jaundice was too busy screaming to feel fully aviophobic. Thankfully, the rug flew out of the truck with them, allowing them a relatively soft landing.

"Oof," said Jaundice, spitting out sand.

"Ouch," said Kale, rubbing her knee where she'd received an unfortunate rug burn.

They looked down at the Nile, and at the truck quickly submerging.

"Whoa," said Jaundice. "Good thing we escaped at the last minute."

"But what about Beatrix?" Kale asked.

The sisters looked down at the river again. Then they looked at each other.

"Beatrix," they both said quietly, taking off their hats. The Bland Sisters observed a moment of silence.

"She was a decent pilot," Jaundice said, finally. "Even if I wanted to throw up each time I boarded her plane."

"What will we do without her?" asked Kale.

"She will be missed," said Jaundice, wiping away a tear.

"Sorely," said Kale, sniffling as she touched her rug burn.

"Who are we eulogizing?" a voice asked behind them.

"A heroic person," explained Kale. "And a good friend."

"I wish I had a chance to know her. She sounds *amazing*," said the voice. The Bland Sisters turned around.

"Beatrix!" they cried.

"I told you girls to jump," she explained. "I find it's wise to take my own advice."

"Now what?" asked Jaundice.

"Now we ride," said Beatrix, giving a whistle. In a matter of moments, her horse was galloping toward them. "Good girl, Cleo."

"Where did she come from?" asked Kale.

"I told you: Omar knows how to get everywhere. And anything," Beatrix reminded her.

"Why don't you tell us what you dreamed about in the garden?" Jaundice asked.

Kale did her best to remember. So much had happened since her dream, it seemed so long ago.

"I was in the desert," she began. "And I saw a mean-looking

man. He was standing on the steps of a weird structure. It had eight sides, and it had a roof, but the rest of it was open."

Beatrix thought for a moment. "Sounds like . . . a gazebo. I bet the man you saw was Victor. And that means two things."

"What?" asked Kale.

"One: He has the other scarab now," Beatrix said.

"And two?" asked Jaundice.

"Your parents are in trouble," said the pilot. "What else happened in your dream?"

"Oh!" said Kale. "He said something about us having something he wanted, and him having something we wanted. And then something about a tomb that's larger than large, and meeting up with 'a queen who was a king,' and 'twins who aren't really twins.'"

"Sounds like a lot of nonsense again," Jaundice said.

"That's what I thought," said Kale. "But now I'm thinking the queen is Hatshepsut, meaning our mother. And the not-really-twins are us. We're supposed to trade him the scarab for our parents!"

"At a tomb that's larger than large?" Beatrix repeated. She thought for a moment. Then her face brightened. "The largest tomb in the Valley of the Kings is the tomb of Seti I."

"That's where Nehy and Nefret were buried," Kale remembered, flipping through her mother's journal. "There's a secret chamber at the end of a long tunnel."

"We'll have to get across the Nile to the West Bank. I hope Omar's cousin doesn't mind transporting a horse on his barge," Beatrix said. She jumped up onto Cleo's saddle, then extended a hand down to the Bland Sisters. "Giddy up, girls!"

"We're supposed to ride on that thing, too?" Jaundice asked.

"You've got to be kidding," said Kale.

Neeeeeigh, whinnied Cleo, shaking her mane.

WHEN YOU TURN, DO IT SMOOTHLY AND CAREFULLY,
SO YOU DON'T DISTURB ANYONE IN THE PLANE.
YOUR PASSENGERS SHOULD ALWAYS COME FIRST.

TAKING OFF! with Trip Winger

❀ ❀ ❀ ❀ ❀ ❀ Chapter Six ❀ ❀ ❀ ❀ ❀ ❀

The Bland Sisters managed not to fall off the horse during their trip over the Nile via Ahmed's barge and across the sands of the West Bank. Also, they seemed to be managing without their sunglasses. Jaundice and Kale considered these major achievements.

The sun was setting as Beatrix and Cleo and the Bland Sisters arrived at the tomb of Seti I, though even in the dusky shadows, the ruins were imposing. A NO TRESPASSING sign hung across the chained gate at the tomb's entry, which was surrounded by all manner of excavating equipment. Beatrix shrugged.

"I've never been one for rules," she said, picking up the handle of a nearby broken shovel. She wrapped the chain around it, then twisted with all her might. Eventually, the chain snapped.

Inside, the tomb was pitch-black.

"Now what?" asked Kale.

"I could make a torch out of this shovel handle, if I had something to light it," said Beatrix.

A small flame illuminated their faces. It was coming from Jaundice, who held out a book of matches she'd pulled from one of her smock pockets.

"They were in a bowl at Ricky's, next to the mints," she explained.

"Brilliant," said Beatrix. "Literally."

"Where do we go now?" asked Jaundice.

Kale took out Hattie's notebook and leafed through it. "Our mother drew this diagram of the tomb, from when she was working with Victor."

Beatrix looked over her shoulder. "I guess we go down these stairs. And keep going down, for a while."

Jaundice held the makeshift torch and Kale held the notebook as Beatrix led the Bland Sisters through the tomb's many corridors and chambers. The walls and columns were covered with beautiful paintings and innumerable hieroglyphs.

"I suppose this is their version of wallpaper," Kale noted, fondly remembering the wallpaper in their bedroom at home—or what was left of their home.

"This 'wallpaper' tells a story," said Beatrix, motioning to one of the walls. "These images are meant to guide the pharaoh safely though the underworld."

"I hope they lead *us* somewhere safe," said Kale, though she had a Feeling it was unlikely.

"So Seti I was the father of Nehy and Nefret?" Jaundice asked.

"That's what our mother's journal says," said Kale. "The twins were supposed to assume the throne, but they died when they were very young, of influenza."

"You mean, they died from the flu?" said Jaundice.

Kale nodded. "They should have just taken some medicine," she said. When the Bland Sisters were sick, they consulted their *Dullsville Hospital Home Health Handbook*, and had medicine delivered in their sundries basket from the Dullsville Grocery.

"It wasn't so simple, back then," said Beatrix. "But at least they had the scarabs, so they'd always be able to visit each other in their dreams. Even after death."

"That's a lovely story," a familiar voice said behind them.

Beatrix and the Bland Sisters turned. They saw a very large and very sharp knife held by a familiar bug-eyed foe.

"Uggo," Jaundice and Kale said at the same time.

"Greetings, ladies," he said. "Fancy meeting you again."

"I knew I should have handed you over to the authorities back in Casablanca," Beatrix grumbled.

"That's the problem with you heroes," Uggo said. "You're too kind."

"Don't worry. I won't make that mistake again," said Beatrix.

"You're right. I doubt you will live long enough," said Uggo. "Now, move it!"

WHEN TWO AIRPLANES ARE APPROACHING
EACH OTHER, BOTH MUST TURN RIGHT TO
AVOID A HEAD-ON COLLISION.

TAKING OFF! with Trip Winger

Chapter Seven

Using his own torch, Uggo directed them down, down, down into the tomb.

"It's quite beautiful," said Kale, until she noticed a vivid mural of twisting snakes.

"I should hope so," said Jaundice. "As it's the last view we might ever see."

Finally, the tunnel opened up into a chamber with two square columns—one featured the image of a boy, and the other featured a girl, both wearing white robes and bejeweled necklaces. They looked more than familiar.

"Nehy," whispered Kale.

"And Nefret," Jaundice added.

Between the columns stood a diminutive man wearing jeans, a denim shirt, and a red bandanna tied around his neck. He was tan, with very white hair, a very pointy nose, and very small, dark eyes, which seemed to glitter as he observed the Bland Sisters.

"That's the man from my dream!" Kale exclaimed.

"Victor Gazebo," said Jaundice.

"Ah," he said. "Smart girls. I'd say you take after your parents, but it turns out they weren't quite as clever as they thought."

He motioned to a shadowy corner. Jaundice and Kale squinted.

At first, the Bland Sisters thought they were seeing another set of hieroglyphs, of a woman and a man with their backs to each other, their hands and feet bound with rope and their mouths gagged. The woman was beautiful, with tawny skin and dark hair, and the man was pale with less distinctive features, though it was clear that he had a determined set to his jaw.

"What does that symbol mean?" Jaundice asked.

"I know I've seen it before," said Kale. "Somewhere."

As she tried to consult her mother's journal in the dimness, the man and woman turned and looked at the Bland Sisters, both of their eyes wide.

"Wait," said Jaundice.

"What?" said Kale.

"The symbol. It just moved," said Jaundice.

Kale looked up from the journal. Her mouth dropped open.

"Mother?" said Jaundice.

"Father?" said Kale.

Despite the gags in their mouths, Hatshepsut Umm and Albertus Magnus Jr. tried to respond.

Jaundice and Kale ran to their parents and embraced them; they smelled of sweat, and of spices. Unfortunately, Hattie and Bert could not reciprocate, as their hands were still bound. But this reunion still managed to bring back another flood of memories for the Bland Sisters.

Jaundice remembered reaching into one of her father's vest pockets and pulling out a thimble. Her father had made the thimble disappear, and then magically pulled it out of her ear, and she had laughed and clapped her hands.

Kale remembered curling up in her mother's lap while her mother read a book. Kale herself could not read at that point, but being in her mother's lap was enough.

And then Jaundice and Kale shared the same memory, of sitting at the breakfast table while their parents fed them spoonfuls of perfectly plain oatmeal and sips of perfectly tepid tea.

It all felt so right, being back together again, the Bland Sisters thought. Even if everything else in the current situation felt very, very wrong.

"What a lovely family reunion," said Victor, smirking. "And how serendipitous that you're all here together, in the burial chamber of Seti I's forgotten children."

"We know all about serendipity," Kale informed him. "This is *not* a good example."

Gazebo laughed. "Not for you, perhaps. Though this can all

end well for everyone, as long as you've brought what I'm after. Do you have the scarab?"

The Bland Sisters' parents started shouting, though what they were saying was muffled. Kale leaned in.

"I think they're saying, 'Don't give it to him!'" she determined. "Though it also sounds a bit like, 'No, isn't it swim!'"

"Once I have both scarabs, I can sell them to a certain very interested and very wealthy buyer. Do you know how much some men will pay for the ability to enter other people's dreams?" Gazebo explained. When he smiled, his teeth were small and yellow, like niblets of corn.

"Is that all you care about?" Beatrix asked. "Money?"

"No," said Gazebo. "I care about power, too." He gestured around. "Consider these pharaohs. For their brief time on Earth, each held the world in the palm of their hand—a world they built on the backs of the weak, the poor, and the servile. I prefer benefiting from someone else's labors, instead of the other way around."

"You're a monster," said Beatrix.

"Well, I'm about to be a very rich monster," said Gazebo. He opened his hand and glared at the Bland Sisters. "Now, enough small talk. Hand it over."

Uggo hovered near Jaundice and Kale's parents, his knife glittering. "Or your mommy and daddy go bye-bye," he threatened.

The Bland Sisters looked at their parents, who were still pleading with them not to do it. They looked at each other.

"Well," said Kale. "There really is only one thing left to do."

"True," said Jaundice.

She reached into one of her smock pockets. She pulled out the scarab. She placed it in Victor Gazebo's outstretched palm.

"Ah," he said, closing his fingers around it. "I knew you were smart girls. Though, sadly, just like your mother

and father, you have also been outwitted, by someone *much* smarter. Uggo, tie them up, please."

Before long, Beatrix and the Bland Sisters were also bound and gagged next to their parents.

"It's fitting, isn't it?" Gazebo said. "You're all about to become permanent additions to this archaeological find. Who knows? In a few thousand years, you might even be worth something."

Then he laughed and flashed his corn-like teeth again. Uggo laughed, too, until Gazebo gave him a stern look.

"Let's go," he said, checking his watch. "I'd rather not keep my buyer—or my bank account—waiting another moment!"

After the two turned to go, the room became pitch dark. Everyone started trying to talk, but the gags on their mouths made it impossible. A few minutes later, a light appeared. It was Jaundice, freed of her ropes and holding a newly lit torch. She pulled down her sister's gag.

"How did you escape?" Kale asked.

"I know all about knots," Jaundice reminded her sister. "Including *untying* them."

"Are we *sure* you're not the older sister?" Kale asked.

"Math doesn't lie," said Jaundice.

Before long, she untied Kale, and then the Bland Sisters untied and ungagged Beatrix and their parents. Jaundice and Kale and their mother and father embraced for a long, long time.

"Oh, how we've missed you," said their mother.

"We've missed *you*," said Jaundice and Kale, tears rolling down their cheeks.

Now that their parents weren't bound and gagged and were illuminated by torchlight, the Bland Sisters could get a better look at them. Their mother was even more beautiful than their vague recollection of her; she did look every inch a queen. Unfortunately, Jaundice and Kale seemed to take after their father's looks, which were significantly less distinguished. But what he lacked in discernible features, their father made up for many times over in other ways, they were sure. Jaundice was particularly happy to see that he was still wearing his trusty vest. It was just as she remembered—though, much like their father, it was slightly worse for wear.

"We tried to meet you in the garden behind the Winter Palace, but the Daughters of Sekhmet got there first, and brought us here," said Bert. "They are terrifying."

"Well, they *were*," noted Beatrix, dusting herself off. "Now what?"

"We need to get out of here," said Hattie. "Follow me back up to the gate."

"Surely, Gazebo's locked it," said Bert, as they all walked back up through the tomb's many corridors and chambers.

"That didn't stop us before," said Beatrix.

"But this might," said Jaundice.

The gate of the tomb was now blocked—not by a lock, but by a huge pile of rubble, no doubt moved there by the equipment outside.

"That horrible man," said Hattie, shaking her fist. "I rue the day I ever met him!"

"Well, if you hadn't met him, you wouldn't have worked for him," noted Kale. "And if you hadn't been working for him, you wouldn't have met our father. And if you hadn't met our father, you wouldn't have had us. *That's* serendipity."

"You've been reading my journal," Hattie said, giving Kale a squeeze. "Good girl."

"I have," said Kale. "And it's given me an idea."

She took the torch from Jaundice and led everyone back to the entrance to the tomb of Nehy and Nefret.

"Your notes say that there's a tunnel that keeps going beyond this chamber," she reminded her mother. "It's supposed to connect the tomb to the underworld."

"That's true," said Hattie. "Though we don't know where that tunnel might take us."

"There's only one way to find out," said Bert.

Hattie looked around the room, then went to a series of hieroglyphs.

"Here," she said. "These markings tell of Sokar. He was the god of the dead, and also the patron of the workers who

built the tomb, and the craftsmen who made its artifacts. The hieroglyphs were left here by Huya, the pharaoh's craftsman."

"Huya was the one who made the scarabs," Kale said.

"That's right," said Hattie.

"I think I just got chills," said Kale.

Hattie stood next to her. "I don't think that's chills," she said. "I think you're feeling a draft. There's air coming from behind this wall."

Beatrix and Bert pushed against the wall with all their might. Eventually, a few of the stones gave way.

"Just be careful," Hattie implored.

"I'll be fine," said Bert.

"I know *you'll* be all right," Hattie said. "I want you to be careful with the wall. This is an important archaeological discovery, after all."

Eventually, Bert and Beatrix cleared out more than a few stones, being careful to place them in piles according to Hattie's direction. When the opening was wide enough, Hattie peered inside.

"There is a passageway," she said. "Though it's probably more of a drainage shaft, to prevent flooding."

"I don't care what it is, as long as it gets us out of here," said Beatrix.

Slowly, carefully, Beatrix and the Bland Sisters and their parents made their way down the drainage shaft.

"This is a lot less exciting than the actual tomb," noted Kale.

"The hieroglyphs are nice and all, but I much prefer these plain gray walls," said Jaundice. Gray was her favorite color, after all.

Eventually, the drainage shaft ended. The rest of the way was blocked by a large pile of stones.

"Looks like it must have collapsed here at some point," observed Hattie.

"This is going to take us forever," Beatrix said.

"Well, we'll just have to work together," Bert said. "All of us."

Everyone lifted and pushed and pulled. A good deal of grunting could be heard.

"I don't know if I've ever carried anything so heavy," admitted Jaundice. "And I'm the one who normally brings in the sundries basket."

"I miss our sundries basket," said Kale, wiping dust from her nose with the back of an equally dusty hand. "What I wouldn't give right now for some perfectly stale bread, perfectly flat soda, and perfectly ordinary cheese . . ."

"We're so glad you girls enjoyed it," said Bert.

"It was the least we could do," said Hattie, "after we left you so abruptly all those years ago."

"It certainly was the least you could do," said Jaundice.

"The *very* least," said Kale, frowning.

Recently, the Bland Sisters had been experiencing a longing for their parents. Now, they were experiencing a new emotion. It made Jaundice's and Kale's faces hot. Their hearts beat wildly. Their hands balled into fists. Their eyebrows furrowed.

"We were all by ourselves for years," said Kale, glaring at Hattie and Bert. "With nothing but a dictionary for guidance and companionship!"

"I can't believe *you just left us!*" cried Jaundice. She picked up a particularly heavy stone and heaved it aside, but even that didn't help.

"Now, wait a minute," said Hattie. "We didn't exactly *abandon* you."

"And you had plenty of guidance and companionship. Don't forget, you had Mrs. Dirge," said Bert.

"Mrs. Dirge, our next-door neighbor?" said Kale. She looked at her sister. Jaundice was still panting, with newfound rage and overexertion. That stone really was quite heavy.

"Before we left, we asked her to look after you," Bert explained. "Good old Mrs. Dirge."

"*Old* is right," Jaundice said. "She died right after you two left."

"Oh, dear. That explains a lot," said Hattie, looking at Bert.

"We're terribly sorry," said Bert. "And we've missed you so very much."

"Can you ever forgive us?" asked Hattie.

The Bland Sisters looked at each other. Eventually, Kale let out a long sigh. "I suppose so," she said.

Jaundice nodded in agreement. She finally seemed to be able to catch her breath, too. Anger was one of their least favorite new emotions, the Bland Sisters decided.

"I always liked Mrs. Dirge," Bert admitted. "She used to darn all of my socks. And all the neighbors' socks, as I recall."

"After she died, we took on her business," Jaundice informed her parents.

"Not to mention her darning egg," said Kale.

"I'm glad you two were able to make the best of things. Your father and I thought we were making the right decision at the time," said Hattie. "It was clear you two were better off at home, until we felt you were both old enough to join us."

"You were probably better off without Mrs. Dirge, too, rest her soul," Bert said. "You always cried when we tried to make you play with other children or babysitters or anyone, really."

"He does have a point," Jaundice said.

"At your age, my parents never let me out of their sight," Hattie said. "It was truly oppressive. I would have loved to be left to my own devices, to discover life on my own terms!"

"We did discover we prefer the white cheese to the yellow. And we're quite proficient in sock darning," noted Kale.

"I enjoy tying and untying knots," Jaundice informed her mother.

"That's . . . not exactly what I envisioned," said Hattie. "But still, a mother can't help feeling proud."

"I'll feel prouder when we've moved this last boulder out of the way," Beatrix said.

Everyone took hold of it, and when Beatrix counted to three, they all pushed. Slowly, it gave way, and a great puff of fresh air wafted through.

The Bland Sisters and their parents stepped out. Jaundice's torch illuminated the sandy landscape, which extended as far as their eyes could see. Beatrix gave a loud whistle, hoping to summon Cleo.

"Where are we?" Jaundice asked.

Bert reached into two of his vest pockets, produced a compass and a map, and considered them. "We're in a valley, it looks like, still west of Luxor. I'm just not sure exactly where."

"There's always Plan M," Hattie reminded Bert. "For now, at least we're free."

"We're already at Plan M?" said Jaundice. "It seems like we were at Plan B only yesterday, when Beatrix came to our rescue in Dullsville."

"That's because it *was* yesterday, darling," said Hattie.

"Time flies when you're having fun," said Bert.

"We might be free, but we're out in the middle of nowhere," Kale reminded everyone. "And Victor Gazebo is about to sell both of the scarabs."

"Well, he does have two scarabs," said Jaundice. "He just doesn't have two *real* scarabs."

"What do you mean?" asked Kale.

Jaundice fished around in her smock pockets. "I bought one earlier today, when we were at the bazaar. It looked so much like the real thing, I thought it would make a nice souvenir. So when Victor asked me to hand over the scarab, I gave him the fake one."

As she handed the real scarab to Hattie, her parents pulled her in for a hug.

"The people of Egypt owe you a great debt," Hattie informed her.

"Well, they're my people, too, right?" Jaundice asked. Her mother nodded, her eyes glistening with tears.

"That's some sleight of hand you pulled there," said Bert. "I think you've inherited some of my family's magician genes."

Jaundice smiled proudly. The Bland Sisters had recently learned about their grandfather, Albertus Magnus Sr., who had been one of the greatest magicians in the world. And they had witnessed more than one extraordinary performance by their aunt Magique, aka the Queen of Magic. So the comparison was quite the compliment.

"What else do you have in those smock pockets?" Bert asked. Jaundice emptied them. She was carrying:

The aforementioned book of matches from Ricky's

A large bottle of sunscreen

A string with several complicated knots tied in it

A handful of date candy, scooped up from the overturned stand in the bazaar

"My favorite candy!" exclaimed Hattie, popping one in her mouth. Kale was glad they were discovered before the smock went into the wash, since she was the one who did the laundry.

"Impressive," said Bert, inspecting the knotted string.

"But now we're back where we started," Hattie said. "We have one scarab, and Gazebo has the other. And his is still about to fall into the wrong hands. If only we knew where he was planning his rendezvous."

"We're going to need reinforcements," said Bert, fishing around in his vest. Eventually, he pulled out a flare gun and fired it into the air.

Jaundice nudged Kale, who had her nose in her mother's journal.

"Stop reading and start helping us think!" Jaundice scolded.

"I *am* helping," Kale said. "And I'm thinking, about the dream I had, where I ran into Gazebo. Remember the last thing he said?"

"Something about queens who are kings and twins who aren't really twins," Jaundice said.

"Right," said Kale. "All this time, I thought he was talking about our mother, and us. But maybe he was talking about a *place*."

She opened the journal to one of their mother's drawings. Hattie's eyes widened.

"The Temple of Amon, in Karnak," she said, nodding.

"A pair of obelisks remains there, but one of them is broken," noted Kale. "Like twins who aren't really twins."

"Constructed by Hatshepsut," added Hattie. "The queen who reigned as a pharaoh."

"That must be it," said Jaundice. She patted her sister on the back. "Sorry I doubted you."

"I might not be almost always right, like you. But I am right sometimes," said Kale.

The quiet desert was soon thrumming with two distinct noises: the sound of hooves and the sound of a car engine. Cleo was approaching from one direction, and Omar from the other.

"I never thought I'd see you again!" he said, jumping out of his car to embrace everyone.

"We need to get to Karnak, to the Temple of Amon," said Bert.

"And we don't have much time," said Hattie.

"My cousin is waiting to ferry us all back across the Nile," Omar informed everyone.

"Giddy-up!" said Beatrix, jumping on Cleo's back.

Chapter Eight

By the time Omar parked his car in the shadow of the Temple of Amon, it was the middle of the night. The ancient sites were closed, the tourists had all gone back to their hotels, and the streets of Karnak were empty.

"It seems so quiet," said Kale.

"Too quiet," said Bert. "You two should stay here with O, while your mother and I look around."

"We're not about to put you in danger again," said Hattie. Then she and Bert scurried off.

"I think we should go with them," said Jaundice.

"But it's safe here, in the car," said Omar.

"O's right," said Kale.

"Yes, but remember what happened last time our parents left us?" said Jaundice. "We didn't see them again for *years*."

"True," said Kale. "Sorry, O. We have to go."

"I don't like it," said Omar. "But I understand. I, too, have parents, and I, too, have never listened to them."

The Bland Sisters crept over to the temple's entrance, and hid behind a palm tree. A car was parked there, headlights on, near where four men stood. The Bland Sisters recognized the silhouettes of two of them.

"Gazebo," whispered Jaundice.

"And Uggo," whispered Kale.

The two other men were wearing impeccable suits and fedoras and sunglasses, even though it was the middle of the night. One was wearing a bright-red tie, and the other was bearded and carried a briefcase.

"Mr. Red, I presume," Gazebo said to the man in the tie. They gave each other the V sign with their fingers. "It's a pleasure to make your acquaintance."

"It should be, given how much I'm about to pay for these scarabs," said Mr. Red, with a thick accent.

"Indeed," said Gazebo, grinning. His teeth seemed even more yellow in the moonlight. "You managed to outbid every other interested party quite handsomely."

"They are worth just that much to me. But how can I be sure that they work as you described?" said Mr. Red.

"They work. Trust me," said Gazebo.

"I trust no one," said Mr. Red. He smiled. "How about we both take a little nap?"

"Here?" said Gazebo.

"We can sit in your car," Mr. Red suggested.

"Very well," Gazebo said. Uggo unlocked the doors, and Gazebo and Mr. Red got in.

"All we need to do is place the scarabs behind our heads," Gazebo explained. "If I appear in your dream, we'll have a deal. Agreed?"

"As long as you or your man don't try to run off with the scarabs and my money," Mr. Red said. He turned to the bearded man next to him. "Make sure they don't try any funny business, Al."

Al nodded and tightened his grip on the briefcase.

"Luckily, I can fall asleep under any circumstances," Mr. Red said.

"I have a fool-proof sleep method," Victor said. "I learned it from my—er, actually, I came up with it, after years of careful research. I just need to close my eyes and imagine I'm floating up, up, up an invisible staircase . . ."

• • •

"What now?" asked Kale. "One of them has the real scarab, but we don't know which one!"

Jaundice thought for a moment.

"I have a plan," she whispered.

"What do I do?" asked Kale.

"Sneak over to the back of the car," Jaundice said, lying down on the ground. "When you hear me yell which one of them has the right scarab, snatch it and start running."

"How are you going to know?" Kale asked.

"Just trust me," said Jaundice, closing her eyes and imagining invisible staircases and velvet, feathered nests.

Kale sighed and did what she was told. After all, Jaundice was almost always right.

But just as Kale arrived at her hiding spot behind the car, she thought she heard a jangling noise. She snuck over to the passenger side and peered in. Inside, Mr. Red was handcuffing Victor to the steering wheel. In her surprise, Kale stumbled back onto the sand. The movement must have caught Mr. Red's eye, because he turned his head.

"Uh-oh," Kale said.

"Kale?" Mr. Red whispered. "Is that you?"

He lowered his sunglasses and leaned down. His eyes looked so . . . familiar.

"Aunt Magique?" Kale whispered. "Is that . . . *you?*"

The Queen of Magic smiled. "Don't worry," she whispered. "We have a plan."

"Plan M," Kale said, remembering her parents' words back in the tomb.

"At your service," said Magique, tipping her fedora.

"Jaundice and I have a plan, too," Kale informed her aunt, whispering the rest of the details.

Just then, the Bland Sisters' parents appeared from the shadows and approached Uggo and the man clutching the briefcase.

"How did you two escape?" Uggo asked. He shook his head. "No matter. Move along. We're conducting business here."

"So are we," said Hattie. Bert produced a gun from his vest and pointed it at the men.

Al raised his free hand. But Uggo hesitated.

"Wait a minute," he said. "Isn't that a . . . flare gun?"

WHAM!

Al swung the briefcase, hitting Uggo in the face. He crumpled to the ground.

"Brava, Albertine!" said Bert, giving his niece (and Magique's daughter) a hug.

"I'm glad *that's* over with," Albertine said, peeling off her disguise. "Though I must say, I was just starting to like the beard."

In the meantime, Victor Gazebo was having the best dream of his life. He was a pharaoh in ancient Egypt, and he was sitting on a golden throne. Beautiful women cooled him with fans. His subjects looked up at him in adoration. There was only one thing missing.

"Has anyone seen a man in a red tie?" he asked. His subjects merely smiled. The women kept fanning.

Gazebo stood up. He looked around. He craned his neck to get a good view of the throne room.

"Mr. Red? I'm over here!" he shouted. "Where are you?"

"I'm right here," said a voice.

Victor Gazebo turned his head to see Jaundice standing right next to him.

"What are *you* doing here?" he asked.

"I'm here to take what's not yours," she said.

The women who had been fanning Gazebo turned into the Lost Twins.

"The Sacred Scarabs of the Twins are both in use," Nehy said. "When they are in use, their rightful owners are summoned."

"Return what you have stolen!" Nefret cried.

Gazebo looked down. The throne was now crawling with snakes.

"*Snakes?!*" he cried, trying to swat them away. "Why did it have to be *snakes?*"

He tried to get up, but he couldn't. The snakes were winding around his arms and legs.

"Let me out! Let me out of here!" he shouted.

"If you insist," said Jaundice. She turned to Nehy and Nefret. "Sorry to have to leave you both like this."

"It is all right," said Nefret. "This is the most fun we've had in ages."

"Literally," said Nehy, smiling.

Jaundice smiled, too. Then she started shouting.

From her hiding spot next to the car, Kale heard her sister calling out to her in her sleep.

"Kale!" Jaundice cried. "It's Gazebo! IT'S GAZEBO!"

Kale scurried over to Gazebo's side of the car. Carefully, she plucked the scarab from behind his head, hoping not to wake him. But just as she was backing away, he opened his eyes.

"The girl! She has one of the scarabs!" Gazebo shouted. He tried to lunge at Kale, but his handcuffed hand pulled him back. Then he turned to Mr. Red for help, but all he saw was Magique, standing on the other side of the car in her impeccable suit, fluffing her hair.

"That 'girl' is my niece," Magique said, smiling. "Clearly, you messed with the wrong family, little man."

"Uggo, the keys!" Gazebo shouted. Unfortunately, Uggo had somehow slithered away from Bert and Hattie and Albertine, and was ready to do his boss's bidding. He got in the car next to Victor and tossed him the keys.

At this, Kale started running. She nudged Jaundice awake along the way.

"Time to go," Kale said.

"Huh . . . ?" Jaundice said sleepily.

"Jaundice! Kale!" Hattie cried. "We told you girls to wait in the car!"

"Would *you* have waited in the car?" Bert asked.

"No, I suppose not," Hattie admitted, as they both started running, too.

Kale caught a glimpse of Omar behind the wheel.

"Omar!" she cried. "Start the car! Start the car!"

Omar did what he was told. Unfortunately, his jalopy chose that very moment to experience engine trouble.

Kale looked over her shoulder. Her mother and father were close behind, as were Victor and Uggo in their car. Magique and Albertine were off in the shadows, attempting to start what looked like a motorcycle. But where was Jaundice?

"Wake up, sister!" Kale shouted. "Wake up!"

Finally, Jaundice opened her eyes . . . to see the headlights of Gazebo's car coming right at her. All she could do was scream and close her eyes again—

—and at that moment, someone grabbed her. It was Beatrix, pulling Jaundice up onto the back of Cleo, who kept galloping.

"Hold on!" said Beatrix. Jaundice did as she was told.

Hattie pulled Kale into the back of Omar's car; from the rear window, she could see Gazebo's car swerve back onto the road and pull up right behind them. Farther back was Beatrix, though Cleo was gaining ground.

"Where to?" asked Omar.

"To the Bluebird," said Bert.

"Can this thing go any faster?" asked Hattie.

"I thought you'd never ask," said Omar. As he stepped on the gas, everyone fell back into their seats.

But Victor Gazebo wasn't about to let them get away. He stepped on the gas, too, and sped right up to Omar's car's rear bumper, which he began ramming with the front bumper of his car.

"He's trying to run us off the road!" cried Omar.

"What do we do?" asked Kale.

"He's trying to run them off the road!" cried Beatrix.

"What do we do?" asked Jaundice.

"We need to get him out of the way, somehow," said Beatrix.

Jaundice fished around in her smock pockets. She pulled out the bottle of sunscreen Ricky had given her.

"I have a plan," she said. "Can you get us in front of the car?"

"You should know by now, I can do anything," Beatrix replied. "Giddy-up, Cleo!"

The horse did as she was told. Soon, they were at the side of Gazebo's car, and then, they were in front of it.

"Here goes nothing!" Jaundice shouted.

She turned and opened the bottle, then squeezed it as hard as she could. A steady stream of goopy white sunscreen splattered all over the windshield. The car swerved to the side of the road.

As Beatrix and Jaundice rode off, Jaundice could see Uggo leaning out the side window, shaking his fist.

"Now that's teamwork," said Jaundice.

VROOM VROOM.

Beatrice turned around. Victor's car was back on the road, its windshield wipers clearing away the sunscreen.

"Oh, no! What do we do?" Jaundice cried.

Beatrix considered the situation. "This one is going to be trickier," she said. "Have you ever ridden a horse?"

"Other than right now?" asked Jaundice.

"All you have to do is hold the reins," said Beatrix. "Cleo will do the rest."

"I'm scared," said Jaundice.

"So am I," Beatrix said. "But we're still going to do this. That's what heroes do. Okay?"

Jaundice swallowed hard. "Okay."

"Good girl," said Beatrix, squeezing the horse's sides. "Giddy-up, Cleo!"

Cleo turned around and headed right for Victor's car. Beatrix met eyes with Gazebo and gave him a wave. He sneered at her in reply.

"Okay, here we go!" she cried. "Remember, hold on tight!"

"Okay!" Jaundice said, gripping Cleo's reins.

And then, Beatrix jumped.

WHOMP.

She landed on the hood of Gazebo's car.

"Going my way?" Beatrix asked him.

"Aaaah!" Gazebo shrieked.

"Gaaah!" cried Uggo.

In his surprise, Victor Gazebo took his hands off the wheel.

LANDING A PLANE TAKES SKILL AND PRACTICE.
WHEN YOU COME DOWN ONTO THE RUNWAY, MAKE SURE
YOU'RE FLYING ACCURATELY AND SMOOTHLY.

TAKING OFF! with Trip Winger

❀ ❀ ❀ ❀ ❀ ❀ Chapter Nine ❀ ❀ ❀ ❀ ❀ ❀

*S*CREEEEEECH.

Victor Gazebo's car swerved off the road—

CRASH.

And flipped over into a ditch.

Jaundice galloped by on Cleo.

"Beatrix!" she cried.

But between the kicked-up sand and the smoke, Jaundice couldn't see or hear anything. All she could do was keep riding.

"Giddy-up," she said. Jaundice held tight to Cleo and her reins as they galloped across the desert, all the way to the riverbank, where Omar's cousin, Ahmed, was waiting with his barge. Omar's car was already there.

"Where is Beatrix?" Hattie asked.

"I don't know," said Jaundice, spitting out sand. "She jumped on Victor Gazebo's car, and then they all drove off the road. It flipped over into a ditch."

Magique and Albertine pulled up on a motorcycle-with-sidecar.

"I think we are now at capacity," Ahmed informed everyone. The barge set off across the river.

"So sorry we're late," Magique said. "This motorcycle needs a serious tune-up."

"I found it by the side of the road," Omar admitted, shrugging. "It was the best I could get for you on short notice."

Kale squinted as she looked at the motorcycle. "That belonged to the Daughters of Sekhmet," she said.

"Cool," said Albertine, holding up a familiar jackknife. "Did this belong to them, too? I found it wedged in the spokes."

"That belongs to Beatrix. She'll be glad to know it's not lost," said Kale.

"I'll be glad to know *she's* not lost," said Jaundice.

"Beatrix is skilled at many things, but especially at staying alive," said Omar, producing a walkie-talkie. "Though, just to be safe, I have already called for an ambulance."

Soon, the barge reached the other side of the Nile, where the Bluebird was waiting.

"We should go," Magique said. "We have a show in Luxor tonight, and we have a lot to do."

"Thank you for your help," Bert said, hugging his sister.

"Anytime, brother," said Magique. "That's what family's for."

"Thanks for the motorcycle," Albertine said, shaking Omar's hand.

"I may not be a magician, but I can make just about anything you need appear," Omar said, offering his business card.

Albertine and Magique hugged everyone goodbye, and then they were off in a puff of exhaust.

"Neither we nor these scarabs will be safe until we can get them to the museum in Cairo, and back in the twins' sarcophagi, where they belong," Hattie reminded everyone. "We have to go right now—we can't wait any longer!"

"Well, we can't go anywhere without Beatrix," Bert said. "Who else is going to fly the plane?"

"I will," said a voice.

Everyone turned around. It was Kale.

"Beatrix showed me how to take off and land. And I've read all of this," she said, pulling TAKING OFF! *with Trip Winger* out of her backpack.

Hattie and Bert looked at Kale. They looked at each other. They blinked.

"Are you sure?" Bert asked.

"Life's not worth living unless we're taking risks and challenging ourselves," Kale said. "Beatrix taught me that. And you did, too."

Her parents hugged her.

"You are *definitely* our daughter," Hattie said.

"Let's go!" cried Bert.

Everyone started getting in the plane. Everyone except for Jaundice. She was bent over now, and breathing heavily.

"What's the matter?" Kale asked.

"I . . . I can't," said Jaundice.

"You've flown before, honey," Bert reminded her.

"And each time it felt worse," Jaundice said. Her eyes were closed now; she couldn't even bear to look at the airplane.

"You just rode a horse across the Egyptian desert," Hattie said. "You thwarted the Daughters of Sekhmet. You outwitted Victor Gazebo, and rescued me and your father."

"And don't forget, you survived kidnapping by an entire crew of pirates aboard the *Jolly Regina* and solved a baffling mystery on the Uncanny Express," Bert said.

"I know," said Jaundice, who was now turning green. "But this—I—I just can't."

"It looks like she's having a panic attack," said Bert.

"It's her aviophobia. That's what Beatrix calls it," Kale said, frowning. "Or *called* it."

At this, Jaundice began to cry.

"What do we do?" asked Kale.

"I could stay here with her, and you two could go ahead to Cairo," Bert suggested.

"And split up again?" Kale asked incredulously.

"No. We're a family. We should stick together," Hattie said. She turned to Jaundice. She put a hand on her forehead. "Honey, I want you to close your eyes."

Jaundice did what she was told.

"Now imagine you're floating up . . . up . . . up . . . an invisible staircase," Hattie said, her voice warm and soothing.

All these years, Jaundice had imagined her mother saying these words—hearing them in person made her relax immediately.

"And into a nest . . . made of feathers . . . and velvet," Hattie continued. Though Jaundice was fast asleep before her mother reached the word *feathers*.

Together, Hattie, Bert, and Kale lifted the sleeping Jaundice and carried her up the stairs and onto the plane. Omar waved to them as they went.

"The ambulance is on its way, and I have just radioed my contact at the police station," he informed them, waving his walkie-talkie. "I will find Beatrix and make sure Gazebo is brought to justice!"

Kale reviewed *TAKING OFF! with Trip Winger* one last time, remembering everything Beatrix had taught her. After she drained the plane's hull and performed a preflight check, she climbed into the pilot's seat and put on Beatrix's cap, goggles, and radio headset. She took a deep breath.

"I have control," Kale said, finally. She yelled "CLEAR" out the window and engaged the starter.

The Bluebird's engine roared to life, its propellers spinning. Kale eased the throttle forward. She checked the instruments and the airspeed indicator.

"All systems go?" Hattie asked.

Kale nodded. She eased back on the stick.

It wasn't the smoothest of liftoffs, but the Bluebird was definitely in the air. That was something, at least. Kale looked back at Jaundice, who was fast asleep in Hattie's arms. She seemed to be smiling.

Jaundice dreamed she was back in the garden of the Winter Palace, sitting on the very bench where she and Kale had fallen asleep the day before. It was a beautiful day, and the gardens were filled with people. Jaundice was pleasantly surprised that neither the bright sun nor the crowds seemed to bother her. Two people in particular looked familiar, and slightly out of place. It was Nehy and Nefret, and they were coming toward her.

"Hello," Jaundice said. "What are you doing here?"

"We had to stop by and thank you, for all your help in reuniting the scarabs," said Nehy.

"We're so glad we don't have to haunt other people's dreams anymore," said Nefret.

"Ugh," said Nehy, rolling his eyes. "Other people's dreams are so *boring.*"

"Helping you was the right thing to do," said Jaundice. "Even if it did almost get us killed, on several occasions."

"You speak about adventure as if it's a bad thing," said Nehy.

"Well, it is fun sometimes, like learning to ride Cleo, and making use of things in my smock pockets, and solving mysteries and thwarting villains with my sister," Jaundice mused. "Even being kidnapped by assassins and trapped in your father's tomb weren't all that terrible, now that I look back on it. I just couldn't get on the plane by myself in the end, though. I was too afraid."

"You were brave in many other ways," Nehy pointed out.

"Sometimes our fears are bigger than we are," said Nefret. "When we were younger, my brother and I were afraid of many things: the dark, dogs, water—"

"And spiders," recalled Nehy. "Don't forget spiders."

"So, what happened? How did you both deal with it?" Jaundice asked.

"We didn't," said Nefret.

"We died," said Nehy.

"Ah," said Jaundice. "Right."

"If only we'd spent less time being afraid and more time enjoying life," said Nefret.

"You're so right," said Nehy.

Nefret nodded. "I almost always am," she said.

"This dream is so much easier to understand than the others I've had," said Jaundice. "It's so nice when everything makes *sense*."

Just then, three figures appeared. It was Hattie and Bert, and they were sitting in the Bland Sisters' old red wagon. Kale was pulling them along at a pretty fast clip.

"Whee!" said Bert, holding out his arms like an airplane.

"Can this thing go any faster?" asked Hattie.

"I thought you'd never ask!" said Kale, giving the wagon's handle a particularly zealous tug.

Jaundice looked back at Nehy and Nefret.

"Well," she said, shrugging. "*Almost* everything makes sense."

"Goodbye," said Nefret.

"Where are you going?" asked Jaundice.

"You've reunited with your family," said Nehy. "It's time we reunited with ours."

"See you on the other side," said Nefret.

"Yes, definitely," said Jaundice. "But not for a while, I hope."

Waving, the brother and sister disappeared. Jaundice looked around. In the distance, she could hear her parents and sister laughing.

"Wait!" she called, running after them. "Is there room in that wagon for me?"

Epilogue

B eatrix was convalescing in Casablanca on the day it arrived.

"I'm perfectly capable of bringing in the mail," she said.

"Nonsense," said Ricky. "You and that broken leg still need to rest."

She flipped through bills and catalogs and all too much junk mail, and then she came to it. A postcard.

Hello! Sorry not to write sooner, but we've been busy. After returning the scarabs to the museum in Cairo, we spent some time visiting all our mother's favorite places, and discovering new things about our Egyptian heritage. Though we still have a LOT to learn about life, we hope you'll agree that we're off to a good start.

Afterward, we decided to take a family vacation, and ended up meeting a secret agent. Fingers crossed that we save the world from destruction.

Hope all is well with you and Ricky—and Paris!

Love, Jaundice and Kale and Hattie and Bert

"It sounds like they're having fun. Doesn't it, darling?" Ricky said, stroking Paris's shell.

Beatrix attempted to scratch under her cast. "When did the doctor say I'm getting this thing off? I'm feeling downright itchy."

"For adventure, I'll bet," said Ricky.

A few months later, and hundreds of miles away, a seagull landed on the bow of a certain ship. In its beak, the bird carried a letter.

"Aw, bless you, Gully," said the ship's first mate, a reformed pirate whose name happened to be Fatima. She whistled. "Captain! We've got mail!"

"I hope it's not another one o' them sweepstakes letters," Peg said. "We never win a bloomin' thing."

"It's from Jaundice and Kale—and their parents!" Fatima said, holding it out for both of them to read.

Ahoy, mateys! Sorry we haven't been in touch sooner—we solved a mystery on the Uncanny Express and helped our parents foil their nemesis in Egypt, and then our family vacation went a bit awry.

  Now we're visiting the Poshworth Museum, where we discovered a cryptic message. It looks like we're in the process of revealing an international conspiracy (while on the run from a nefarious adversary). Wish you were here!

  Love, Jaundice, Kale, Hattie, and Bert

"Blimey," said Peg. "Sounds like they got tired of reading about adventures, and wanted to have some of their own."

Fatima held the letter to her nose, and inhaled. She shared it with Peg, who did the same.

"Mmm," they both said. "Spices."

Later that year, backstage at the latest stop on their blockbuster world tour, Magique and Albertine were relaxing after their latest show. A stagehand brought them two more flower arrangements from adoring fans, along with a package. Inside was a set of souvenir Academy Award salt and pepper shakers, and a letter.

Greetings from Hollywood, California! Everything here is as dramatic as you might imagine. In fact, a crime has just been committed at the Noir Diner, and the police don't seem to be doing anything to solve it. We'll surely need a break from our travels after this little escapade!

Love, Jaundice, Kale, Hattie, and Bert

"Hollywood," said Albertine, sighing. "I've always wanted to go there."

"Who says we can't?" said Magique, raising an eyebrow.

Miss Penny Post was exhausted. It had been some time since she'd assumed the role of head (and sole employee) of the Dullsville Post Office, and she hadn't had a single day off. Fortunately, she loved her job, unlike her predecessor, Mr. Bartleby.

In the mornings, she spent her time sorting the incoming correspondence; she enjoyed seeing letters and packages from far and wide, especially since she herself wasn't afforded any

vacation time. On this day, she found the sorting particularly diverting, because one particular envelope was addressed to Miss Penny Post herself. Inside the envelope was an invitation.

YOU'RE INVITED!
WHAT: A HOMECOMING PARTY
WHO: Jaundice, Kale, Hattie, and Bert
WHERE: Our house, on the road to Dullsville
WHEN: This Saturday, anytime you're able
HOPE TO SEE YOU THERE!

"Saturday?" said Miss Penny Post, glancing at her calendar. "Why, that's today."

Carefully, she finished sorting the mail. Then she grabbed her hat and coat. She looked around.

"See you tomorrow," she said. Though she was the only one in the office, it seemed like the polite thing to do. As she left, Miss Penny Post put a sign she'd made on the door.

CLOSED, it said, FOR POSTAL HOLIDAY.

By the time Miss Penny Post arrived at the house on the road to Dullsville, the party was already in full swing. Pirates, magicians, and other intriguing-looking characters were in attendance—even Mr. and Mrs. Crumb, the owners of the Dullsville Grocery, were on hand—after all, they had delivered the Bland Sisters' sundries basket all those years. Today, they supplied the flat soda, as well as the day-old bread and cheese for the party sandwiches.

Fatima was singing one of her latest sea chanties, while Peg accompanied on a hornpipe and kept time with her wooden leg. In the kitchen, Kale and her mother were preparing more food, and Kale was instructing Hattie on the pros and cons of cutting one's cheese sandwiches vertically vs. horizontally as her mother made notes in her new journal. Aunt Magique and Bert were sitting on the couch, performing card tricks, while Jaundice was teaching Omar how to tie her favorite knots. Beatrix and Ricky and Albertine were all trying to coax Paris out of her shell.

"Oh, Miss Penny Post! We're so glad you came," Kale said.

"I'm so glad you invited me," said the mail carrier. "This is quite a crowd."

"Wait until you meet the others. They'll all be here soon," Kale informed her.

"Let me take your coat," said Jaundice. It was not as usefully pocketed as her smock, but she did admire the stitching.

"The house looks much better than it did the last time I saw you," Miss Penny Post said.

"It did need quite a bit of cleaning," Kale said with quite a bit of enthusiasm.

"And new furniture," added Jaundice.

"It must feel nice to be home, finally," Miss Penny Post said.

"It does," said Jaundice. "Though it's only temporary. We're off again in a week."

"Where to?" asked the mail carrier.

"It's a secret, I'm afraid," said Kale.

"Well, it's a shame you're leaving so soon," Miss Penny Post said. "I know how much you two love being at home."

"We still do," said Jaundice.

"That's the thing about families," Kale said, looking at her sister. "Wherever we are, we're always at home."

"I'll drink to that. Actually, we should *toast* to that," said Jaundice. "I'll pour soda for everyone."

"I'll help. Be right back," Kale said to the mail carrier. "In the meantime, try the sandwiches. The cheese is perfectly ordinary."

Miss Penny Post agreed. The cheese really was perfectly ordinary. And though the bread was perfectly stale and the soda was perfectly flat, it was all perfectly complemented by the lively music and company. In its own way, Jaundice and Kale's Blandness was endearing. It was certainly enduring.

And it was, however unintentionally, entertaining.

❀ ❀ ❀ ❀ ❀ AUTHOR'S NOTE ❀ ❀ ❀ ❀ ❀

E ach Bland Sisters story has been its own unintentional
adventure for me as a writer. *The Jolly Regina* was my
very first middle-grade novel. *The Uncanny Express* was my
first mystery. *Flight of the Bluebird* is my first novel set in a
real location, and featuring a real (and very rich) culture and
history, all of which I wanted to present in an accurate and
respectful way. From early on in the process, I knew I would
need a special crew to get this bird off the ground.

I am so fortunate that James P. Allen, Wilbour Professor
of Egyptology at Brown University and past president of
the International Association of Egyptologists, generously

volunteered his time and energy to talk with me and review all-too-rough drafts of my manuscript. Professor Allen was able to provide information about the logistics of traveling in Luxor, archaeology and the ethics of its practice, and fascinating details of Ancient Egypt, many of which I used and some of which I fictionalized. (For instance, there really was a passage discovered not too long ago in the tomb of Seti I, but it ended up going nowhere, and he never had twin children who communicated via magical scarabs. And though Sekhmet is a real Egyptian warrior goddess, I'm afraid there is no real-life gang of international biker-assassins who wreak havoc in her name.) Professor Allen's wife, Susan, also a well-traveled archaeologist, also lent me her expertise. I am grateful for their wisdom, and for the fact that they happen to live just a few blocks away from me here in Providence, Rhode Island— as the Bland Sisters would say, talk about serendipity.

I must also thank Julia Boyce, who referred me to pilot Allyn Copp. I am grateful to Allyn for reviewing all of the aeronautical details in *Flight of the Bluebird*. (I would have used his real name in the story, but "Trip Winger" seemed a bit more fitting.)

In addition, thanks as ever to Barry Goldblatt, agent extraordinaire and baggage handler; Tamar Brazis, daredevil editrix; the fierce gang at Abrams/Amulet; Jen Hill, a craftsperson whose magic would make even Huya jealous;

and goddesses and friends Anika Denise and Jamie Michalak, who helped me excavate this story from several ruinous drafts. And of course, I could not have done any of this without the copilots of my heart, Scott and Camden, who continue to inspire me to new heights.

Speaking of inspiration, we are all fortunate that heroes like Bessie Coleman, Amelia Earhart, and Nellie Bly existed and persisted, but I am particularly thankful that there is so much material available about their lives, which is manifested—or rather, *womanifested*—in the character of Beatrix Airedale. If you want to hear about real-life women who faced great adversity and had incredible adventures, I suggest you go out right now and learn about Beatrix's historical foremothers. You can thank me later.

It pains me to say goodbye to Jaundice and Kale, though I hope our paths cross again one day, however unintentionally. Creating them and their stories has been the hardest, most fun thing I have ever done—so far, at least. I hope these Bland girls have entertained you, and perhaps even encouraged you to seek some adventure yourself. As a wise woman once said, "Life's not worth living unless we're taking risks and challenging ourselves."

ABOUT THE AUTHOR

Kara LaReau was born and raised in Connecticut. She received her master's in fine arts in writing, literature, and publishing from Emerson College in Boston, Massachusetts, and later worked as an editor at Candlewick Press and at Scholastic Press. She is the author of The Unintentional Adventures of the Bland Sisters series, illustrated by Jen Hill; *Ugly Fish*, illustrated by Scott Magoon; The Infamous Ratsos series, illustrated by Matt Myers; and *Goodnight Little Monsters*, illustrated by Brian Won. Kara lives in Providence, Rhode Island, with her husband and son.

ABOUT THE ARTIST

Jen Hill is the illustrator of The Unintentional Adventures of the Bland Sisters series by Kara LaReau; *Diana's White House Garden* by Elisa Carbone; and *Doing Her Bit: A Story About the Woman's Land Army of America* by Erin Hagar. She is also the author and illustrator of *Percy and TumTum: A Tale of Two Dogs.* Jen is a graduate from the Rhode Island School of Design, where she studied children's book illustration with David Macaulay and Judy Sue Goodwin Sturges. She lives in Brooklyn, New York, with her husband and her intern, Little Bee, who is very helpful for a cat.